KNOW
SMOKING

(a unique info-novel)

The Whole Truth About
Smoking and Quitting

Simon Bryant, MD

Cartoons by
Vance Rodewalt

Middle
Way *PUBLISHING, Inc.*

MiddleWay Publishing, Inc.
P.O. Box 70008 (BPO)
Calgary, Alberta
CANADA T3B 5K3
e-mail sbryant@telusplanet.net

10 9 8 7 6 5 4 3 2 1

Canadian Cataloguing in Publication Data

Bryant, Simon, 1958-
    Know smoking: the whole truth about smoking
and quitting

Includes bibliographical references and index.
ISBN 0-9681456-0-4

    1. Tobacco habit. 2. Smoking. I. Title.

HV5740.B79 1997   613.85   C96-901038-9

Manufactured in Canada

Illustrations	Vance Rodewalt
Cover artwork	David Anderson / Image Setters, Calgary
Layout	Abbie & Jim Swanson / www.digitalbanff.com
Printing	BEST, Toronto

Typeset in Times Roman and Papyrus

acid free paper

20% post consumer

Dedicated to children everywhere.

- *Ten percent of the author's proceeds is pledged to educating people in developing countries about tobacco abuse.*

- *A further ten percent is pledged to Child Haven International, a registered charity which provides for destitute orphans in India and Nepal.*

- *Two trees will be planted for each one used in the production of this book.*

Please Note

Although this book is based on a careful review of the medical literature, new information is continually becoming available. The reader is strongly urged to consult a licensed health practitioner before acting on the information herein, with respect to smoking or using tobacco or nicotine replacement in any form. The author and publisher cannot be held responsible for any errors, omissions, or outdated material. They specifically disclaim any liability for injury, loss, or damage incurred as a direct or indirect consequence of the use and application by you of the information and suggestions in this book. The names and characters in this work are fictitious unless otherwise specified.

CONTENTS

Acknowledgments

This book would never have seen ink without the assistance and encouragement of many others who freely lent their time, knowledge, skills and support to make it all possible. In particular, the production team deserve special mention: Abbie and Jim Swanson (layout); Vance Rodewalt (cartoon renderings); David Anderson of Image Setters, Inc. (cover art); Sally Banks (editorial assistance); Paula Duncan (indexing). Thanks also to Tom Milutinovic of Pennan, Inc.

Vance Rodewalt deserves special mention. He once drew for Marvel Comics and is now editorial cartoonist at the Calgary Herald. His creations over the past thirty years include the syndicated cartoon *Chubb and Chauncey* and two books of his own work, *A Brush With Irreverence**and *With Weapons Drawn.** I am privileged that he contributed his talent to this work.

The chapter-opening quotes are mostly from *Wisdom of One: the ultimate existentialist quote book* by Thomas E. Kelly (ISBN 1-883697-42-5, Hara Publishing). The cartoon on page 64 is from the Archives of the National Library of Canada, item 1990-492-1010.

Finally, too many individuals to list here provided critical review of the work-in-progress, and gave the finished project their endorsement. I am profoundly grateful for their encouragement and support.

Any credit for this book belongs to all those referred to above. Any errors or offenses are my responsibility.

* (available from Temeron Books, Inc.)

Introduction

The truth about smoking has been twisted around and covered up for too long. Tobacco is in movies, on billboards, in our history and in our literature. It almost seems to be part of our culture. Almost "normal." But there might be more to it than meets the eye.

As a physician, the more I learned about the effects of cigarette smoking and the history of the tobacco industry, the more outraged I became. It's a scam, really. As the American Medical Association has concluded, the public has been "duped."

I wrote this book because I believe that people have a right to know the whole truth, and to enjoy the freedom of informed choice. People may choose to smoke or not, but too often they don't know what the contract they're signing is about. The truth has been suppressed. It's time to get the facts straight.

Perhaps you're a veteran smoker with years of experience, or perhaps you never took a puff in your life. In either case, I hope you learn something from Joe K. Hamel, his wife Robin, and Dr. Borenot. I did. It's not impressive numbers that count, of course, it's you. So please take what you want, and leave the rest.

Know Smoking contains useful information for smokers and those who are involved with them. It's also about caring for others, having fun, and making decisions based on facts rather than on advertisements and other illusions. Knowledge is power.

Finally, I'll ask you to take whatever you learn from this book and share it with the children in your life. They deserve the information that too many others, now addicted to nicotine, were denied.

Thank you.

1

Smelling Smoke

Men perish because they cannot join the beginning with the end.

— Alcarnaeon

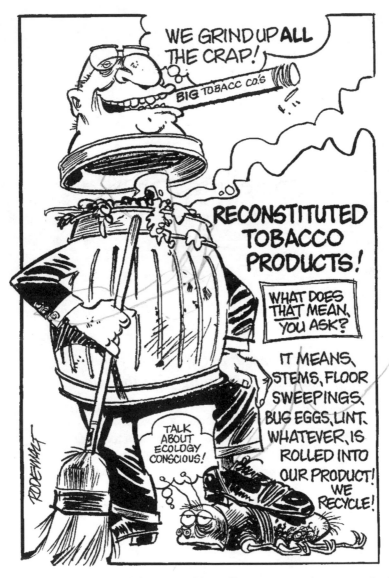

(*Author's note:* Check for a list of ingredients on your cigarette pack...)

December 30th

"WOULD YOU MIND IF I SMOKE ?" Mr. Joe K. Hamel immediately asked when Dr. Robert Borenot introduced himself and extended his hand in greeting.

"Of course," the doctor answered without hesitation, and they shook hands.

"Thanks," Joe said, and then lit his cigarette with a flourish of a solid-gold lighter.

Dr. Borenot was reported to be some kind of expert on how to quit cigarettes. Joe had expected a total ban on smoking in this office. He'd even imagined himself walking out, in protest.

Wait a minute, did the doc's "Of course" mean *of course he minded,* or *of course Joe could smoke?* As a figurehead for a major tobacco company, Joe had developed a subtle paranoia and an appreciation for half-truths. He quickly scrutinized the doctor's face, meeting a friendly gaze.

Joe had money and freedom enough to spend his time as he wished, and he seldom denied himself a compulsive pleasure. Smoking was as much a part of his high-flying lifestyle as the company jet, his frequent holidays, and his familiarity and comfort with real financial power. After taking a deep haul on his cigarette he said "I really don't want to quit, you know." Gray-blue exhaled smoke mingled with his emphatic words.

"You don't want to stop smoking right now. Perhaps you never will," said Robert, with a hint of a shrug. He motioned to a couple of executive chairs on either side of a low table, and Joe and he sat down without a word.

Robert waited for Joe to speak.

"Yeah, I believe in smoking. It's good, for me. But you know, next week is New Year's. Maybe you can suggest a suitable resolution or something?"

Robert reached for a clean ashtray from his nearby desk, and placed it within Joe's reach. "Perhaps," was all he said about that before changing the topic. "Give my best wishes to Robin, by the way." Robert had helped Joe's wife Robin to quit smoking, almost three years before.

Joe was puzzled by Robert's deflection of his question. The doc was in no hurry, it seemed, sitting comfortably with his hands resting on the arms of his chair.

"I certainly will. She sends her regards, too. And she fairly insisted that I talk with you," Joe added.

He'd come to this meeting for two reasons other than to satisfy his wife's concerned demands. The first was Robert's curious business card, which simply read 'Robert Borenot, MD. How to Smoke Correctly, private consultations.' The second reason was an undiagnosed cancer tickling the back of his throat.

The tumor had been discovered just ten days before, after a trip to the doctor about a blocked ear that wouldn't clear. Nobody could say what kind it was, but it seemed to be progressing quickly.

After the initial shock of learning about his disease, Joe had put up his usual defense: out of sight, out of mind. But there'd been a whole series of tests and discussions with perplexed specialists who raised more questions than they could provide answers for. Christmas had been a bitter celebration. Now here he was at their recommendation, spending his precious time with this evasive anti-smoker.

Joe tossed Robert's business card on the table. "What's this about smoking correctly?" he asked. "That's ridiculous. You must be kidding."

"I do sometimes kid around, Mr. Hamel. You'll see what

I mean by smoking correctly, if we choose to work on it together. By the way, what would you like me to call you?"

"The name is Joseph K. Hamel. Also known as *'Joke Hamel.'* Joe is fine though."

"Why 'Joke,' Joe?"

"Oh, I guess I like a good laugh. People take things too seriously." Joe hesitated, then admitted somewhat ruefully "Let me tell you though, I haven't laughed much since getting this disease."

"Yes, I was sorry to learn of your illness, Joe. Let's hope for the best."

"Amen, Doc."

"You can call me Robert, if you wish."

"Good. Now tell me, what exactly have you got to offer?" Joe asked, suddenly very businesslike.

"I've developed a special program to help people quit smoking. It's different from anything ever tried before," said Robert. "I've given up family medicine to concentrate on this project. You see, in the part of town where I used to practice, about a third of my patients smoked. Since every second smoker will die of some disease caused by their habit and lose an average of 15 years from their life expectancy, I decided to see what I could do to help."

"Every second smoker loses 15 years?" Joe asked.

"That's the current situation in North America. And something like 8 out of 10 smokers will be smoking again within one year of quitting. We can do better than that."

Joe interrupted with a dismissive wave of his hand. "What's the use of trying to get people to quit, if you don't mind my asking? What's the use of me quitting?"

Robert preferred that his clients reach for their own conclusions, rather than having him lead the way. He remained silent, letting Joe take the initiative. He got the message.

"Okay, I'd like to hear about your method," Joe said. "Do you use any particular technique?"

"I use a variety of approaches. Information, humor, hypnosis, handouts, whatever seems best. In about 14 sessions we'd cover most aspects of smoking."

"Fourteen sessions? Kind of long, isn't it?"

"Stopping smoking takes time, Joe. Most people make about five attempts before they finally succeed. Preparation and perseverance are important."

"What's so special about your program, Doc?" Joe demanded. He puffed quickly on his cigarette before continuing more diplomatically, "I hope my questions don't bother you, by the way. I think for myself, and speak my mind."

"No problem, Joe. Say or ask anything you want. I don't think of myself as some kind of a teacher or an expert. I just help people figure things out for themselves."

Robert then sprang a gentle trap.

"I like to think that my method relies on a person's own wisdom and judgment," he said, "so it might work particularly well for you."

Joe smiled, unconvinced but now seriously interested. "What exactly is involved?" he asked. Like many people who smoke, he needed information before inspiration.

"Some hypnotic suggestion. Information handouts. I also encourage my clients to complete certain assignments from time to time. "

"Hypnosis? That doesn't really work, does it?"

"Well, I just read about a fascinating experiment in which smokers wore headphones while anesthetized for surgery. One group heard recorded suggestions to quit smoking, and another group heard only music. Three months later, those in the 'suggestion' group were more likely to have quit, or to be smoking less."

Joe sat forward in his chair. "Really? Quitting should be simple, then, a piece of cake. A little hypnosis and hey, presto, you're a non-smoker!"

Robert shook his head.

"Unfortunately, not exactly. Hypnosis is really just a strong form of suggestion," Robert said. "Its effectiveness depends on how receptive the patient is. I mostly use it to help people relax and concentrate."

"Sounds interesting anyway. But what's to stop you from controlling a person's mind like that?"

"Everything. I certainly can't make anybody do anything that goes against their basic beliefs or morals. Think of hypnosis as a strong recommendation, if you prefer. Would you like to try it, and see for yourself?"

Besides a no-smoking policy, Joe hadn't been sure what to expect from this first session. A boring lecture, perhaps; certainly nothing quite so mesmerizing.

"I don't know, Doc." He finished the last of his cigarette, stubbing it out slowly and staring at the ashtray for a few seconds. "What have I got to lose? Like I said though, I really believe in smoking."

"That's all right. We won't be dealing with your smoking today, just testing how well you take to hypnosis. Let's make you the caveman who discovered tobacco."

"The *what*?"

"Relax, Joe. Remember, you're the boss, and you stay in control. Sit back and enjoy this. Most people do."

Joe settled back into his chair, discovering a lever on the side to adjust the angle of recline.

"Take a few deep breaths, Joe. Just notice your breath flowing in and out as though it had a life of its own. Forget your body for a while. Follow your breath in and out." Robert continued talking in soft, measured tones.

"You'll be able to respond when spoken to, and laugh or react in any way that seems natural. Afterwards you'll remember everything about this experience.

"Now imagine that you're living in the 'PreZippoLighter' period, during the early evolution of our species. There are no cars of course, no gas barbecues, and no lighters. You have fire though, and crude stone weapons which you use for hunting and defense. Life is a constant struggle for survival. Wild animals can attack at any time.

"You're about four feet tall, Joe, and very hairy. You walk around sort of stooped over, as if carrying a heavy weight on your shoulders. But you're no slouch as a hunter, and can recognize an opportunity when you see one. You and your buddies scour the countryside for small animals, or occasionally gang up to take down a sickly mammoth.

"Are you with me, Joe?"

Joe nodded and grunted in response. Obviously the hypnosis was effective.

"It's a particularly dry year, and game is scarce. After mulling it over amongst yourselves you decide to travel in search of better hunting. The camp is packed up, and the last thing you need to bring along is the fire. You wrap some glowing coals in a bunch of green leaves and set off.

"Fire is wonderful. It's warm. The flames prevent you from becoming the hunted at night. What's more, if you haven't caught anything for awhile you can always order a pizza by smoke-signal."

Joe smiled at the ridiculous image and Robert continued, satisfied that his client wasn't sleeping.

"After several days of fruitless search, you set up camp in a patch of dead, dry tobacco plants. The vegetation gives off a musty, sweet smell. You've never seen such a plant before, but you're all much too exhausted to investigate the novelty or even give it much thought.

"The next morning you carefully wrap some embers from the campfire in several leaves of the air-dried tobacco. They smolder into life and the fire quickly spreads. You catch a few breaths of its noxious fumes, choke, turn a sickly green, and pass out.

"Now you dream that you're riding effortlessly through a hunter's paradise on the back of a swift camel. Big, fat, sleepy mammoths are everywhere. Your terrible hunger has been replaced by a vague nausea, quite an improvement under the circumstances."

Robert paused to collect his thoughts. He had some idea of his client's personality from first impressions and what he'd learned while treating Robin. He knew about Joe's position in the tobacco industry, and that he'd developed an unknown illness. Beyond that, the man was a mystery to him.

The imaginary account continued, a spontaneous creation of Robert's imagination.

"You regain consciousness to find that your comrades have extinguished the blaze and are watching you intently. You feel cool, relaxed, satisfied, lucky, and about as sexy as a prehistoric person can be.

"You grunt reassuringly to your worried companions, something to the effect of 'Hey, check this out. Me tobacco-man now!' They fashion some crude cigars from the strange new plants, and the age of smoking begins.

"You live to the ripe old age of 32 before succumbing to a massive heart attack. Now imagine that from the vantage of those happy hunting grounds you once dreamed of, you can watch as history unfolds before you."

Robert studied the man in the recliner. Javaman-Joe looked peaceful, breathing softly with his head rolled slightly to one side. The lines on his face had smoothed out. Evening shadows darkened his right cheek. Somewhere in there, Robert knew, a cancer was growing.

"A few centuries pass by as you watch the future human race develop. The population quadruples, there are traffic jams on the main trails, and food becomes scarce due to over-hunting. People begin to cultivate their food and keep a few domestic animals.

"Smoking catches on like nothing ever before and by five hundred years after its discovery, about half of all adults and many children are using tobacco regularly. Despite suffering severe coughs and a decline in lung power, nobody seems inclined or able to stop.

"Your distant descendant Javaman incorporates the world's first tobacco company, JavaBacco, to take full advantage of the situation. They monopolize tobacco cultivation and distribution. Since money hasn't been invented yet, their product is traded for seashells, food, animal hides, and foot-rubs. Foot massage is a big hit because nobody has any shoes. Business is fantastic.

"Are you still with me, Joe ?"

"Sure am, Doc," Joe mumbled.

"Okay, now imagine that you're a researcher at that point in history, diligently seeking something to compete with tobacco on the global market. You analyze various plants by inhaling the smoke they produce when burned.

"One day you test a coffee bush. The effect is so disgusting that you immediately toss a bucket of swamp water on the smoldering plant.

"Have a look around you, Joe."

Joe opened his eyes then, seeing the office in a most unusual light. The potted plants were towering palms, the comfortable chairs were conveniently-shaped boulders to sit on, and the walls were made of woven reeds plastered with mud. An overhanging cliff formed most of the roof.

Robert sat across from him, clad in animal skins and

sporting a matted beard. He reached out and offered Joe half a coconut shell filled with a prehistoric brew. Joe accepted it in both hands and took a tentative whiff.

"The brown liquid dripping through the burnt leaves and roasted beans collects in a pool on the ground," Robert suggested. "On second sniff, you consider that perhaps the smell of the stuff is more appealing than the smoke was appalling. In the spirit of scientific inquiry, you taste it. Fantastic — you've created the world's first freshly-brewed coffee."

Robert observed that Joe was sipping excitedly from his coconut coffee cup. He was exceptionally hypnotizable.

"Congratulations Joe! Your discovery is a milestone in human evolution and coffee bars soon spring up at every trail junction. Now close your eyes again and relax."

Joe put down his cup and sat back, listening intently.

"JavaBacco recognizes a real threat to their profits and responds with their secret weapon, advertising.

"The creative marketing people at JavaBacco develop many effective techniques. They give away clothes and other items branded with the JavaBacco name. Cartoon characters, smoking of course, are painted on large boulders to appeal to children. Cigarettes are freely distributed at rock concerts. The Roling Stones are very popular.

"JavaBacco sponsors the Mammoth-Mile Drag Race and the world's first golf tournament. Players have to carry their own clubs and stay off the racetrack, of course. The very respected Sabretooth Symphony Orchestra gets a new enclosure, and a fresh conductor every week."

Joe didn't react, so Robert then probed a bit further.

"Meanwhile, JavaBacco's researchers discover some fascinating properties of nicotine. It passes from the lungs to the brain in just seven seconds, for example, and may relieve anxiety, boredom, and minor depression. They soon realize that it's a highly addictive drug, and that tobacco smoke is very harmful to one's health. The top executives of the company, telling each other they need more proof of the truth, decide to conceal this information from the public."

Joe stirred and his forehead tightened as though he were concerned about something. Robert ended the hypnosis.

"Joe, you'll wake up when I snap my fingers, and be able to remember everything that you've experienced."

Robert snapped his fingers and Joe looked around as though waking up from a vivid dream. Then he laughed.

"Wonderful," he said. "That was really enjoyable." He seemed more relaxed, and receptive. "How does it work?"

"It's just your own imagination, Joe."

"That's fascinating. I can still see those coffee shops springing up in the primordial jungle, complete with expresso machines made from bamboo." Joe thought for a few moments "But you know what? I don't think that coffee would really provide much competition for tobacco."

"Why is that?" Robert asked.

"Simply because there's nothing quite like a cigarette with coffee. The more coffee people drank, the more cigarettes they'd smoke."

Joe was a master of marketing, Robert thought.

"They do go together well, Joe. Smoking may even cause the body to break down caffeine more rapidly. Coffee drinkers who try to quit smoking might think that nicotine withdrawal is causing their anxiety, sleep disturbances, heart palpitations, and irritability. Too much caffeine could also be to blame, though. A person who quits smoking should probably cut his or her caffeine intake by about half."

"Well, that's news to me. I guess I've learned something today. But I'm no closer to wanting to quit, after listening to your crackpot theory."

"Crackpot theory?" Robert exclaimed, feigning indignation. "There's plenty of evidence to support it! Firstly, there are traces of fire-carrying behavior in the tradition of the Olympic torch. Secondly, companies like JavaBacco are doing very well today."

Joe chuckled, shaking his head.

"For example," Robert continued, "Philip Morris is just one of the major tobacco companies. Annual sales for this company alone were over $50 billion way back in 1992, with almost half of its $4.9 billion profit coming from tobacco sales. After buying Kraft and General Foods, Philip Morris became one of the ten largest corporations in the United States. Tobacco is serious business."

Joe stared hard at Robert, not quite able to make out his intentions. "You're no fool," he said.

"And neither are you, Joe. So shall we test your lungs?"

"What, right now?" said Joe, seemingly startled by the sudden change of subject and perhaps by the prospect of more bad news.

"Sure. It's easy. As the National Lung Health Education Program suggests, test your lungs and know your numbers."* Robert retrieved a compact office spirometer from his bookshelf and set it up. "Just blow into this mouthpiece as hard and as long as you can."

Joe filled his lungs, exhaled forcefully as instructed, and then coughed hard, several times. Once he had his breathing back under control Robert suggested that he try again.

"Perhaps you've loosened some of the mucous in your chest with that coughing. You might be able to improve on these results," he said, examining the graph and printout.

Joe repeated the test.

"That's only slightly better," said Robert. "And you're still a long way from normal."

* "Test Your Lungs / Know Your Numbers" is the motto of the National Lung Health Education Program.

"Is that bad?" asked Joe.

"The way I look at things, Joe, it's good."

Joe stared at him, uncomprehending.

"It's good because there's still breath in your body, and room for improvement."

Joe chuckled. "So my lung numbers are down but the big number isn't up? I like your attitude," he said.

"Good," Robert said. "And how about *your* attitude? Do you think we can work on it together?"

"I don't want to quit. I can't commit myself to 14 sessions," said Joe. "Things are a bit uncertain."

"Of course. We'll take one step at a time, and you can stop whenever you wish."

Does he mean stop the sessions or stop smoking? Joe wondered. *This fellow has a fascinating way with subliminal suggestions.* "Would every session be like today's?" he asked while thinking that if so, this approach wasn't for him.

"Oh no. We'll often have more discussion, and there'll be assignments to review from time to time. Today I just wanted us to get some sense of how receptive you are to new ideas. I know you don't want to quit. Perhaps I can help you *want to* want to, though."

Joe looked straight at Robert for a few moments. "Want to want to? Yeah, okay," he said, catching on. Now that suggestion seemed to fit the bill! "I'll give this a try."

Robert smiled. "Congratulations, Joe. Now our time is almost up, so here's your first assignment. For next week I'd like you to make up a theory of the origins of smoking. Include the facts that smoking is a major cause of male impotence, and reduces fertility in women. While you're at it, find out the statistics on a few other health consequences of smoking."

Joe's jaw dropped slightly before he answered "Sure. I can do that little bit of homework."

"Incidentally, anything you say in this office is completely confidential," Robert said.

They agreed to meet in a week's time.

"Happy New Year, Joe," said Robert as he saw his client out. "And give my regards to Robin."

"I sure will, Robert. And Happy New Year to you, too." With that, Joe left.

* * * * *

Robert made a note in Joe's chart, summarizing the situation.

Mr. Joseph Hamel is a 42-year-old tobacco company figurehead who has developed an unknown and possibly very aggressive cancer. He made it quite clear today that he does not want to quit smoking; He is certainly in the "precontemplation" stage of quitting, and may never change. For now it's important not to jump ahead. My objective is simply to increase his perception of the risks of smoking, and of the benefits of quitting. Perhaps he'll see things differently in a few months. That cancer complicates the matter. At this point he may be motivated more by fear than by hope.

For next week:

Joe's assignment: create a story about the effect of smoking on sexual function. Research the health consequences of smoking.

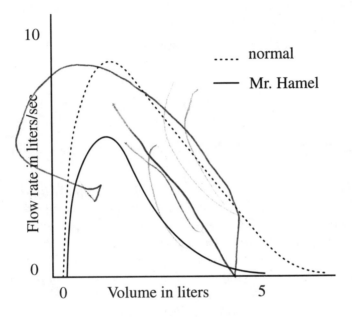

Mr. Hamel's spirometry results showed
quite severe changes. How about yours?

2

Not Getting Burned

The great enemy of the truth is very often not the lie, deliberate, contrived, and dishonest, but the myth, persistent, persuasive, and unrealistic.

— J. F. Kennedy

January 6th

NEW YEAR'S HAD COME AND GONE, and already many resolutions only five days old would have crumbled under the force of habit. Robert collected his thoughts in the gray Monday evening as he waited for his client to arrive. Their second meeting could be a turning point, he knew. Joe might either continue the journey of change that he'd begun the week before, or stay stuck, building his defenses stronger and higher.

Joe arrived and Robert welcomed him warmly, wishing him all the best in the New Year. Joe dropped into his seat and willingly accepted a fresh cup of coffee. The two men exchanged small talk for a bit, impressions of the wintry weather and the commercial corruption of the season.

"I usually escape from it all, take off to somewhere hot," Joe said, "and I still might." He spoke briefly about this year being different, certain issues at work and his doctors wanting him around for tests, but offered nothing important about his experiences over New Year's week.

Following their first session Joe had left the office intrigued by Robert's unusual style. For three consecutive nights after his hypnosis, he had dreamed that he was living in prehistoric times.

For the first two nights he returned triumphant from the hunt, but on the third he slipped at the crucial moment. The beast at bay turned on him and Joe had woken up in the dark, fighting for breath and clutching at his wounded throat.

"I'd like to see what you've come up with about the health consequences of smoking," Robert said, to introduce the day's work. "and I want to hear your theory about how smoking got started. But before we begin, may I first ask you a few questions about your past health?"

"Of course," Joe said. He drew and lit a cigarette as Robert prepared a notebook and pen.

"When did you take up smoking, Joe?"

"I was fifteen or so. My whole family smoked and it seemed a natural thing to do. I think my folks might have been surprised if I didn't. Granddad was a tobacco farmer and it probably runs in our blood." A diamond ring flashed as Joe tipped the ash from his cigarette into the ashtray.

"And about how much have you used over the past six months, daily? Two packs?" Robert had a habit of suggesting a figure higher than the average, knowing that people tended to underestimate and underreport their smoking.

"About two packs a day, more or less," Joe agreed. Robert looked up from his writing with each question.

"And have you ever tried to stop smoking, or to cut down? Or even thought seriously about it?"

"Never." It was as simple as that.

"Do you use any other tobacco products, such as cigars, or snuff?"

"I do enjoy the occasional cigar. I really do. But I don't care for snuff."

"And what kind of cigarette do you usually smoke, Joe? I mean what strength?" Ratings of nicotine content vary between cigarettes, Robert knew, with the strongest brand available supposedly having several times as much nicotine as the weakest. This would make a difference when considering the use of nicotine replacement, such as the patch or gum; dosages might require some adjustment.

Robert continued to gather the essentials of a brief smoking history, touching on the use of other drugs and alcohol and general lifestyle habits. His doctors had prescribed asthma medications for his lungs. He was in reasonable health, apart from his cancer and some lung damage from smoking. His family history was unremarkable, from a medical point of view. In short, he had been a successful and very fortunate man until recently.

"You've smoked for your entire adult life and you don't think that there's much point in quitting," Robert summarized. "You might think it's too late now to change. You don't feel that smoking harms you, though you know that it has." Carefully chosen words. "Perhaps you're right."

Joe stared at him, not sure he was hearing correctly.

"You're basically a perfectly normal smoker, Joe. About 80% of smokers in America today were using tobacco regularly by their 18th birthday," Robert said. "Seventy percent of them say they want to quit, but even more than that have no specific plans to do anything about their smoking."

Joe had gathered his wits by now.

"No, Robert. You don't understand. I like to smoke and I don't want to quit. But I suppose I can't continue." He looked pointedly at Robert. "Did you ever smoke?"

"For twenty-five years, Joe. When I was twelve, a helpful friend offered to share his cigarette. It was a wretched creation of recycled Butt-bacco that he'd scavenged from ashtrays. Truly awful! Gave me the worst headache and nausea of my life. I figured I must be doing something wrong, so I went out and bought a pack of smokes. No instructions inside, though.

"That was before the package warnings. Anyway, they just say 'Smoking Kills,' or something equally pessimistic. Nothing at all about how to smoke. Many smokers are still alive, so the packages must lie."

"Doc, are you for real?" Joe objected. "Actually, even I know that smoking is harmful, and addictive."

"So they say, but are you sure they aren't mistaken? During the Great Bubonic Plague, schoolboys would be beaten if they didn't smoke each morning. In the 18th century, patients with blocked-up intestines were treated by blowing tobacco smoke into their rectums.

"Relax, Joe," Robert said, noting his client's bewildered expression. "I'm not Abbas the Shah of Persia."

"Who? You're losing me."

"Abbas was a radical anti-smoker during the seventeenth century. Rumor has it that whenever he learned of any nearby camel-train loaded with tobacco, he'd have his soldiers burn the cargo and cut off the ears and noses of the camel drivers. I think that's going a bit too far."

"Uh, just a bit, Doc," Joe said. Robert's curious pronouncements had caught him a bit off-balance.

"Joe, let me make myself clear. These days there's a lot of emotion around smoking, and a fair bit of moralizing. There's no right or wrong about it, though. People are free to choose their poison, so to speak. I don't have any right to judge another person's life." Robert said. "You can remind me of that anytime you wish. Does that make sense?"

"It sure does." said Joe, somewhat relieved. "Now I can appreciate what you're saying."

"I'm not trying to lay some guilt trip on you. My goal is to make sure that you understand everything you need to, about tobacco and smoking."

"Thanks again, Doc. What's the most important thing?"

"The most important? Well, you wouldn't try to make your car go around a corner by getting out and pushing sideways on the fender, would you?" Robert suddenly asked.

"Certainly not if I were sober," said Joe.

"Right. You'd get behind the driver's seat, take control, and steer your way around the corner. It's the same for quitting smoking. If you use some knowledge and strategy you'll get much better results, faster."

Joe nodded and settled back in his chair. This process might take some time, but it sounded promising.

"Now, how was your week?" Robert asked.

Joe chose to describe his three dreams, rather than the events of the previous few days. "What do you think they mean?" he then asked.

"You went hunting successfully, twice, but then you became the victim. Perhaps the message is that what once worked for you won't work any more."

"I don't know. Could it be that simple?"

"It's however you see it, Joe. Dreams are personal. Did anything particularly unsettling happen last week?"

"Yeah. I started that assignment." Joe reached into his briefcase and handed over a single sheet of paper with three lists, entitled *The Health Consequences Of Smoking:*

Cigarette smoking is responsible for:
- one third of all cardiovascular disease and strokes.
- one third of all deaths from cancer.
- 90% of all lung cancers and most emphysema.
- sickness and even death in children of smoking parents.
- at least 1/3 of all deaths between the ages of 35 and 69.

This means that:
- At least 1,000 Americans and 100 Canadians die every day from smoking.
- 50% of smokers will die of a smoking-related disease, about 15 years too soon.
- About five minutes of life are lost per cigarette smoked.

Major conclusions:

- Nicotine in cigarette smoke is an addictive drug.
- Smoking tobacco causes a whole lot of preventable disease and death.
- It's possible to quit smoking.
- Quitting improves your health, and life expectancy.

"That's a great little summary, Joe. Tell me, what do you think of that information?"

Joe shrugged as if to suggest that it wasn't important. "It's just a few facts lifted from United States Surgeon General reports, and a few other sources. I already knew most of it," he added.

"What about the rest of the assignment, then?"

"Oh, you mean my special theory about how smoking began? I've got it here somewhere." Joe fished in his briefcase and produced his trophy.

"Great. Would you please read it to me, Joe?"

Joe cleared his throat a few times, at least once for real. Robert pivoted his chair about and put his feet up on the desk, leaning back with his hands clasped behind his head. Joe stood and announced his conclusions slowly and precisely, as though he were addressing a large and attentive audience. He was a showman at heart.

"Ladies and gentlemen, it's thought that smoking evolved in a steaming swamp that was swarming with disease-carrying mosquitoes. Smokers would be surrounded by a cloud of tobacco fumes which protected them from the deadly insects. As a result, they tended to survive longer than non-smokers and so could produce more children.

"Eventually smoking evolved as an instinctive human

behavior, with newborn babies bumming smokes soon after taking their first breath."

A smile crossed Robert's face. "Very interesting," he commented, "but can you prove it?"

"This theory has been criticized for two reasons," Joe continued. "Older male smokers are more likely than non-smokers to be impotent, and smoking also reduces fertility in women. So it might not have been such a great strategy after all, in evolutionary terms.

"On the other hand, there are still fiercely-defended *Smoking* and *No Smoking* zones in the modern world, territorial claims of the descendants of smoking and non-smoking tribes. There's also some vague scientific evidence that nicotine addiction can be inherited.

"Ladies and gentlemen, these questions are clouded with controversy. You will simply have to judge the smoking facts for yourselves," Joe concluded. "Thank-you for your attention. And may I wish you all good luck."

"You've done some research," said Robert. "I've never heard of nicotine addiction being passed on to one's kids. At least not through DNA, that is. Would you mind bringing me the reference?"

Joe chuckled. "You think that's possible? You really think that people might smoke because they're programmed to by their genes?"

"Well, it's conceivable." said Robert. "If the urge to smoke isn't partly inherited, then where does it come from?"

"Why, it's a matter of free choice," said Joe. "Nobody forces anyone to smoke."

Robert said nothing for a few moments. There was usually no point in arguing with that kind of statement, but he sensed that Joe would prefer an honest reaction. He looked steadily at his client.

"That argument is a red herring in an ocean of deceit," Robert eventually said matter-of-factly. Joe didn't bat an eyelash. "For now, why don't we focus on why *you* smoke? I'd like you to consider that. Whenever you find yourself smoking, make a note of one possible reason why."

"Sure. That should be interesting," said Joe, quite sincerely. "That would be useful information." He paused, with one hand on his throat. "Those statistics are a bit of an eye-opener," Joe said, motioning to his assignment lying on the table. "Of course I knew that smoking was harmful, but…"

They left it at that, sharing the silence. Before Joe left, they agreed to meet weekly for the next three months.

Robert watched from his window as Joe crossed the cold, empty street. A few flakes of snow sifted down like ash from somewhere in the sky.

Joe reached for the keys to his car. He found the door already open and felt a chill run down his neck. Was it the winter breeze? He was certain that he'd left it locked. After looking cautiously inside, he settled into the luxurious vehicle and started the motor.

When it came to life, Joe pulled away.

* * * * *

Robert completed his entry in Joe's clinical record:

Joe has a forty to fifty pack-year history of smoking, and has never seriously considered stopping. Today he seemed willing to acknowledge some of the harsher facts about smoking. He might be moving into the contemplation stage, wanting to want to quit.

On the other hand, I can't quite make out whether he's preparing to quit smoking or hopes to carry on as before. Time will tell.

Joe's homework: monitor his smoking

3

Forbidden Fruit?

To die is poignantly bitter, but the idea of having to die without having lived is unbearable.
— *Erich Fromm*

January 13th

ROBERT LEAFED THROUGH HIS NEWSPAPER while he waited for Joe to arrive. The weather had stayed as gray and uninspiring as the news through the previous week, and showed no sign of imminent change. Each day opened with an incomplete lightening of the gloomy darkness, and closed with its return.

A court had ruled that a ban on tobacco advertising was illegal. Rumor had it that a Southeast Asian dictator, responsible for the slaughter of a quarter of his country's people, had not died by a bullet but of malaria. A refugee camp in the Middle East had been bombed by supersonic jet fighters.

Life was returning to abnormal. All that remained of the spirit of Christmas was the occasional tattered decoration. The celebration and the sales were ending, and the hangover was well under way.

Joe eventually appeared in the doorway, gray-skinned and tired. He seemed a bit unsteady as he hung up his coat, and his speech may have been a bit slurred as he greeted Robert.

After taking his seat Joe produced a bottle of whiskey and two crystal tumblers from his briefcase, and placed them on the table. "Season's greetings?" he asked, indicating the liquor. Was this some kind of test, Robert wondered? A gesture of trust? Alcoholism?

Robert stood away from Joe's invitation but took the two steps needed to briefly place a hand on his shoulder. "Thanks for the offer," he said. "Maybe we'll share a drink later. We have some work to do right now," he said.

Work to do, indeed. Sometimes it seemed the whole world was burning, and here was Joe fiddling his time away.

"Something bothering you today?" Robert asked.

"Yeah. They say my disease is quite serious."

The news from his doctors was that the tumor appeared to be malignant and spreading. They still really weren't too sure though; there was somthing very unusual about it.

Robert and Joe discussed the new development. At first Joe seemed inclined to believe that he was doomed to a swift demise. That might have been true, but there was still some reason to hope. Joe could live for another forty years, or two. Until a firm diagnosis was made, the jury was out.

"I guess time will tell," Joe said eventually.

"That's good, Joe. That's a good perspective. Maybe you can beat this problem."

That was Robert, always the optimist. Never satisfied with less than the best effort that he could make, he patiently expected as much from others.

"Yeah, but I wasn't able to beat smoking," Joe said. "What can I do against cancer?"

That's odd, Robert thought. Something about Joe's statement raised a red flag. He had said last week that he'd never tried to stop smoking, ever, but now he spoke as though he had. Robert knew he probably wouldn't get anywhere asking about the inconsistency directly. Was it simply a reluctance to admit failure, he wondered, or something else? Joe seemed unusually defensive about his habit.

"You can only ever do your best, Joe. Whether it's trying to quit smoking or struggling with a serious cancer, you can only ever do your best. You may not be ready to boot the smoking monkey off your back just yet. Of course, you do stand a better chance, without it."

Joe grinned when Robert put it that way.

"I like that. I'm not the problem, the monkey is. He isn't me," Joe said.

"That's right, Joe, but right now the question is why do you smoke? The monkey seems to be holding the leash and the collar is around *your* neck. Let's do something about it. Shall we look over that last assignment?"

To Robert's evident surprise Joe produced an impressive collection of napkins, parking stubs, and other scraps and pieces of paper from his briefcase. "I just wrote down my ideas on anything that came to hand." he explained.

"Brilliant!" Robert said. "Just read a few of those at random, then."

Joe selected a restaurant napkin. "After a meal, to digest better," he read. From a parking stub, "while driving, to stay awake." A coat-check ticket: "during intermission at a concert. Craving." And so on, as a comfort, a boost, entertainment, a ritual, a sedative, a drinking companion. Perhaps even as a friend, a reliable partner. Stress relief. Just a habit.

Once Joe finished his litany of reasons, he asked Robert why most other people smoke.

"There are plenty of reasons, Joe, but the main one is simply nicotine."

"You don't think that smoking is a substitute for the memory of breast-feeding?" Joe asked with a smile. "It seems that smokers tend to have been nail-biters and thumb-suckers, in comparison with non-smokers."

"Really? Where did you learn that?"

"From the Internet." Joe had no trouble finding information about tobacco and smoking, on the World Wide Web. Smoking had become a public as well as a personal issue. Tobacco was making the news.

"I even ordered a videotape about what makes people smoke" Joe said.

"What's it like?" asked Robert.

"I don't know. I haven't had a chance to watch it."

"Let's check it out, then."

Joe nodded and reached for his briefcase to produce *The need for nicotine; a presentation by Professor I. Knowtall, running time 8 minutes.*

Robert took the tape and loaded it into a video machine on the bookshelf, then opened one section of the wall unit to reveal a small television set. He settled back into his chair with the remote control in his hand.

Professor Knowtall flashed onto the screen and proved to be a burly, loud-spoken fellow. The video showed him lecturing to an invisible audience.

"Ladies and gentlemen, about a quarter of all North American adults smoke, and younger men and women continue to adopt the practice. Why is this? Firstly, the pain of smoking is delayed for many years. Secondly, nicotine is addictive. Finally, people don't know the facts about smoking.

"Let's consider that many of the consequences of smoking develop gradually. There's aching legs, impotence, angina, infertility, premature aging, emphysema and disabling shortness of breath, asthma in one's children, chronic bronchitis, osteoporosis, broken bones, and so on. I won't bore you with the details.

"The consequences steadily increase in number and severity. Some of the results of smoking might seem to occur abruptly, but they are really the result of ongoing exposure to tobacco smoke. There's strokes, for example, heart attacks, fatal house fires, and SIDS."

"SIDS?" Joe interrupted.

Robert punched the pause button on the remote control. "Sudden infant death syndrome," he said. "The most common cause of death in infants between the ages of 1 month and 1 year, in North America."

"I know," Joe said. "I know. What's smoking got to do with it?"

What's going on here? thought Robert. Then he remembered in a flash that Robin and Joe had lost their third child as an infant.

"Smoking during pregnancy or around an infant has recently been linked to SIDS, Joe." It was bitter medicine to administer, but effective.

Silence smothered the room for several long moments. Professor Knowtall stood suspended in mid-sentence. Joe blinked several times. He stubbed his cigarette into the ashtray. *A rather long butt,* Robert noticed. The video screen flickered, waiting to continue its testimony.

"I guess I sort of knew that," Joe said. "Let's see the rest of this. The man might have a point."

The professor came to life again at a push of a button.

"I don't think that anybody would smoke, if all those problems happened with the first few packs, instead of years later. I've never known an ex-smoker who regretted quitting, but I've met countless smokers who bitterly regret ever starting. The small pleasure of a cigarette is immediate, but the anguish is delayed. I think that's the main reason why people smoke at all.

"My second point was that nicotine is addictive. For example, one study reported that 40% of surviving smokers were smoking again, within two weeks of leaving the hospital after their first heart attack. Ladies and gentlemen, nicotine hijacks the soul.

"Finally, most people who smoke know the taste, but not the poison. Public education is pitifully inadequate, and people still don't understand the consequences of

smoking. By and large, the public still thinks lung cancer is the main danger of smoking. In fact, ladies and
gentlemen, smoking is responsible for one half of all
deaths between the ages of thirty-five and sixty-nine,
one third of strokes and heart disease, a third of all
deaths from cancer, and ninety percent of all lung cancers and serious lung disease.

"As far as the individual smoker is concerned, here's
a chart showing the risks:"

Risk of Dying From Smoking:

Lung cancer	1 in 6
Heart disease	1 in 8
Emphysema	1 in 19
Stroke	1 in 33
Other diseases	1 in 6
Combined risk	**1 in 2**

Life lost, per smoker killed:15 years*

"You can see that there's more than one way to die
from smoking.

"In summary, I suggest that there's three reasons
why people smoke: there's a long delay between the
pleasure and the pain of smoking, nicotine is addictive,
and people underestimate the risks. Tobacco may be a
tempting type of 'forbidden fruit,' but I say — let it rot
in the fields. I'd like to thank you now for your attention, and turn the microphone back to our chairman."

The recording ended there, in a blizzard of white noise
and static.

*table from *Smokescreen* by Barry Ford, Halycon Press,
 Australia, 1994, p.204, paperback edition

Joe stared at the empty screen for several seconds, his mind full of unanswered questions.

Robert waited for a few moments. "I know you lost a child to SIDS, Joe," he said gently. "Don't blame yourself. You and Robin didn't know. We don't have all the answers."

"Yeah. I guess. Damn it." Joe reached for another cigarette, paused, then looked at Robert wonderingly.

"But what makes *me* want to smoke? That pedantic professor didn't exactly answer that question."

Robert pointed out that people smoke for different reasons at different times, as Joe had discovered from his assignment. Because it feels good. Peer pressure. To take a risk. As a kind of medication. Because it's forbidden. For stress control. In a misguided attempt to control their weight. To relieve anxiety and boredom.

"But it does feel good to smoke," Joe said. "Sometimes." They discussed this and other rationales and justifications for smoking.

Feels good? Of course. The proof of that is in the pattern. People don't repeatedly hurt themselves on purpose, but will go back again and again to something they enjoy. And for the nicotine addict, relieving withdrawal symptoms by smoking can be a distinct pleasure.

Peer pressure? Teenagers may start because it helps them to feel relaxed and accepted among their friends, who smoke because it allows them to feel relaxed and accepted among *their* smoking friends. Like, everybody smokes, right? You know, it's great to be one of the crowd.

What about smoking for the thrill of tempting fate? One pack per day really is far more dangerous than say, airshow stunt-flying, or scuba diving regularly. Smoking is a high-risk sport! The lifetime odds of dying from it are 1 in 2, compared to perhaps 1 in 10 for consistent airshow flying and 1 in 125 for intensive scuba diving.

Robert explained that smoking is far and away more dangerous than having high blood pressure or high cholesterol. "Imagine playing Russian roulette with a bullet in every second chamber of the revolver," he said. "It seems that 50% of smokers will eventually die prematurely. They're either attracted by the risk or they don't know the odds. They gamble beyond their means."

Tobacco as a medication for anxiety and the blues? When compared to non-smokers, people who smoke tend to be more downhearted. They drink more alcohol, and may feel helpless in the face of challenges. Depressed people and schizophrenics are more likely to smoke and to have difficulty quitting, in comparison to those in good mental health.

Joe wasn't at all satisfied with these explanations.

"No, what the heck is it that makes me smoke? I don't even notice lighting up sometimes. And that SIDS thing. I don't know. I still don't want to stop. What *is it* about nicotine?"

"Let's talk about nicotine next week, Joe. It's getting late." It had been another short session, but Joe had more than enough to think about. They'd covered plenty for one day.

"Thanks. I guess you're right. Do I have another assignment?" Joe asked.

"Yes, your next assignment is to make up some really unhelpful advice for smokers."

"You mean helpful advice, don't you?"

"No. *Unhelpful* advice, Joe. Now, I seem to recall an invitation and surely the session's over for today." Robert eyed Joe's bottle, noting the brand. "Lagavulin. My favorite single malt whiskey."

They shared a toast to better times. Joe savored the way Robert seemed to accept him: smoke, tobacco career, alcohol and all.

The winter evening light faded from the day, casting dark shadows into the room. Robert whistled a few bars of music, and then began to sing softly:

I first used nicotine, when I was just a kid,
and what a stinking, mean, and nasty thing it did.
Smokes burned me up inside: what horror had I lit?
Although I almost died, I found I could not quit!

Joe laughed, and applauded briefly.

My God, it was no joke, to dance addiction's beat,
craving tobacco smoke, and dragging on my feet.
I thought I'd met my match, and that I'd come to harm,
until I bought "the patch," and stuck it on my arm.

It took me seven quits; the nut was hard to crack.
Cigarettes are the pits, a monkey on your back.
I'm smoke-free once again, and living is so sweet:
no more tobacco-brain, down on Nicotine Street.

"Bravo! What's that little ditty called?" Joe asked.

"The Tobacco-Brain Blues. My very own composition."

"Very original, Robert. I like that 'Nicotine Street' image. It sounds fashionable, you know. Glamorous. Smokers might go for it."

Now Robert laughed. "Sure, Joe. Do you think smokers are any different than non-smokers?" he then asked.

"I don't know. No, I guess not," said Joe.

"We share a few fortunate years on this planet together," Robert continued somewhat philosophically. "We laugh, we cry, we think, we struggle, we learn, and finally we pass away. And we take a lot for granted, don't you think?"

Joe adjusted his position. He looked hard at Robert. "I guess so," he said, and lit a cigarette. He liked this still unfamiliar fellow. Maybe he really could get a handle on his smoking, his cancer, and his entanglement with tobacco.

They parted after the one shared drink.

It was dark and cold outside, and snowing ashes again. Still, tomorrow was another day. Perhaps there'd be some blue sky, at some point.

* * * * *

Robert made his usual chart entry:

Joe is on track. He showed up with a bottle of liquor and an invitation to share a drink. I thought this was strange behavior for a session with a therapist, but then he demonstrated real interest in learning more about his smoking. He even brought in a video on why people smoke. I'd say he's in the "contemplation" stage now, thinking about quitting but not sure how and not really ready to. Sadly, I remember that he and Robin lost a child to SIDS and he learned today of the connection with smoking.

Medically he might not be doing very well; the cancer could be more serious than he feared.

Joe's assignment for next week: create some unhelpful advice for smokers.

4

The Soul Of A Cigarette

*One is healthy when one can laugh at the
earnestness and zeal with which one has been
hypnotized by any single detail of one's life.*
                                        — Nietzche

January 20th

WHILE WALKING TO HIS OFFICE Robert noticed how the sun reflecting off a white wall had melted back the ice on the sidewalk. Even in the midst of winter there were inklings of warmer times. Sparrows went about their bird-business ruffled by the lethal weather, but never ceasing to strive for survival.

Joe arrived for his fourth session, hung up his coat, and sat down in his usual place. His doctors *still* didn't know what kind of cancer he had, he reported, and he was feeling extremely anxious about it. They talked about that for a while, then moved on.

"Any other concerns today, Joe?"

"Yeah. Don't get me wrong. I appreciate your efforts," Joe said, "but I don't feel much closer to stopping."

"Patience, Joe. Quick success is often followed by quick failure. Remember that about 85% of smokers who quit without adequate preparation will start up again within one year. The long-term regular tobacco user is an addict, and quitting is a serious undertaking."

"So, you think I'm a nicotine addict," Joe stated.

"Who cares about the label?" Robert responded. "Call smoking a habit, or an addiction, or normal, or whatever. It doesn't matter what you call it. The point is, you want to enjoy a reasonably long and satisfying life. On the other hand you probably won't, if you continue smoking. Let's focus on that. Forget the labels."

Joe was silent.

"You and what you make of your life are what matters," Robert emphasized.

Joe nodded, getting the point. "Sure, Robert. But like I said, I still don't really want to quit smoking."

"That's okay, Joe. That's where you're at right now. Bear with me, and the motivation will happen. You can't suddenly want to quit; you have to build up to it by seeing where smoking fits in your life and personality, and finding substitutes for nicotine.

"Don't forget, nicotine is the real reason that you smoke. I want to cover that today. But first, you've probably spent some time on your assignment. Shall we have a look at it?"

With a hint of a smile, Joe handed Robert his creation:

A good example of some bad advice
(basic first aid for smokers in withdrawal)

A desperate smoker will do almost anything for a cigarette. Watch for a pleading expression, pouted lips, and two fingers held to the lips as if smoking, all signs of severe nicotine withdrawal. Addicts in real trouble may make a slitting motion across their throats, like scuba divers signaling that they're running out of air.

This is a medical emergency. You must respond immediately. Every second counts. Exhaled smoke contains the nicotine, vaporized tar, and other wonderful stuff that smokers would die for. You have to get some of your spare smoke into their lungs, quickly.

Blowing smoke in the victim's direction is not good enough. The precious fumes would then be diluted and polluted with clean air! The victim needs a full-strength hit of tobacco smoke.

Sharing your cigarette or simply giving the victim one can create more problems than it solves. For one thing you will have less smoke for yourself. Furthermore, such generosity only supports dependency. In the worst case, an addict can endanger their rescuer by panicking and not passing the cigarette back!

A safe, effective rescue method exists. Simply transfer your exhaled smoke to the casualty through a rolled-up tube of paper. Cardboard centers from toilet-paper rolls work very well, if available. Direct mouth-to-mouth resuscitation is a last resort, because of the risk of infection. Not to mention the taste.

Congratulations! You've saved a life.

Robert placed the paper on the table between them.

"You completed the assignment perfectly, Joe. That's *definitely* unhelpful advice. But why so sarcastic and bitter?

A ripple of irritation across Joe's face betrayed his reason.

"Damnit, Robert, this whole thing is frustrating me. I live to smoke, but it's killing me." And others around me, he thought. "I can't stop. I feel like such a fool sometimes."

"You feel helpless," said Robert. This is getting too heavy, he thought. "You ought to be ashamed of yourself."

Joe sat up in his chair, caught sight of his reflection in Robert's words, and laughed. "Yeah, I get it. Stick to the facts, right? No sense getting frustrated before I know all the facts. So tell me about that nicotine-monkey," he said.

"I'm sure you already know the essentials of nicotine, Joe. I could certainly review them if you wish, but it might be more useful for you to *experience* them. Would you be comfortable with another session of hypnosis?"

"Sure, as long as I don't have another nightmare like after the first session," Joe said.

"No guarantees about that, but I'll do my best."

"Great. I'll go for that."

"Okay. Sit back and relax, Joe. Close your eyes." Robert

spoke for about five minutes, inducing a deeper and deeper trance in his patient. "Feel free to participate," he eventually instructed Joe, when he was well hypnotized. "You'll be actively involved in our discussion.

"Now Joe, imagine that you're a scientist in your lab, studying rats to find out what parts of their brains are stimulated by food and other rewards. You train them to press a lever to obtain food, or water, or sex, and they quickly learn the task.

"Your research involves inserting tiny electrodes into the animals' brains to measure what's going on there. All goes well, until one day you accidentally get one rat's wires crossed. Now, instead of the usual reward, every time this particular rat presses the lever it receives a tiny shock to a specific part of its brain.

"The poor animal goes absolutely haywire. It prefers to repeatedly press that lever rather than have food, water or sex! You watch, horrified, as the animal begins to show signs of exhaustion. You suddenly come to your senses and disconnect it from the stimulating electrode.

"You immediately consult a colleague who is an expert in addiction medicine. Here, take the call."

Robert drew his cell-phone from his briefcase, selecting a speed-dial number. He then placed it in Joe's hand. The phone on Robert's desk rang. He answered it, assuming his best imitation of a woman's voice.

"Addiction Research Center. Dr. Cynthia Waters."*

"It's Joe Hamel, Cynthia. Something rather extraordinary has happened." Joe went on to describe his serendipitous discovery in more detail.

"That's incredible," Cynthia said. "That electrode must be in some sort of reward center in that animal's brain."

"Does this explain addiction?" Joe asked excitedly.

*fictitious names

"Perhaps brain surgery will eventually prove to be an effective treatment for addiction?"

"I doubt it," Cynthia said. "Addiction is an interaction between a reward, a person's problem-solving skills and strategies, and their circumstances. The reward can be something that feels good or just less unpleasant, such as relief from stress or withdrawal symptoms."

"But how exactly is addiction defined?" Joe asked.

"It's a situation whereby the drug use or behavior is obviously harmful, but the addict continues anyway. Physical dependence may develop, meaning the addict requires more to achieve the same effect. And there are withdrawal symptoms if the drug isn't used regularly."

"According to that definition, my rat isn't really addicted to the stimulation," Joe said.

"That's right. That's not an addiction in the human sense, Joe. We're much more influenced by our environment and circumstances, than your rat seems to be. For example, some American soldiers who used heroin regularly in Vietnam had little difficulty stopping when they returned. People who use narcotics for relief of pain seldom become addicted to them. Addiction isn't an automatic consequence of using a potentially addictive drug."

"I see your point, Cynthia. I doubt that my rat is aware of what's happening, in the way that a human can be," Joe said. "Addiction is starting to make some sense to me. Say, thanks for your help, Cynthia."

"It's a pleasure, Joe. And by the way, let me know what else you discover. I'm very curious to know what part of that rat's brain is involved. That was quite a lucky strike, I must say. You've come a long way in your research."

"I'll keep you posted, Cynthia. And thanks again. Goodbye for now."

"Goodbye, Joe," Cynthia said, and hung up. Joe placed the cellular phone on the table.

Robert resumed his normal tone of voice.

"You eventually learn that the rat was being stimulated somewhere near the medial forebrain bundle, part of the brain that's involved with pleasurable sensations. You think you're about to make a major discovery with a few more experiments, but then your government research grant isn't renewed.

"A tobacco company approaches you with a very attractive offer. They want you to study nicotine for them. You think about it, and accept."

Robert paused. Should he continue? Joe seemed comfortable. What would be in his client's best interest?

"Tell me what you would discover about nicotine and smoking, Joe, in your work for the tobacco company."

Joe coughed, shifted in his seat, and cleared his throat.

"Nicotine stimulates parts of the brain associated with reward and pleasure," he said. "For a person who is dependent on the drug, smoking can be just as rewarding as drinking when thirsty, or eating when hungry. This is because repeated exposure to nicotine changes the human brain, over time. We know from autopsies that regular smokers develop more nicotine receptors in their brains. There must be a constant supply to fill these greedy little receptors, or withdrawal symptoms occur."

Robert sat frozen in his chair. He'd instructed Joe to just be himself, but then also suggested that he was a researcher. There seemed to be some kind of crossover between the two. It was quite strange. Joe was now speaking with authority as *himself*, from his own knowledge. Should he interrupt the hypnosis, Robert wondered?

"Nicotine is a potent, versatile, fast-acting drug that can

serve as a stimulant, sedative, or poison," Joe said. "It can increase a person's concentration and briefly relieve the blues, or settle jangled nerves. Did you know that biologists once used concentrated nicotine in capture-guns to tranquilize wild elephants?"

"No, I didn't," Robert quickly answered. "No wonder cigarettes can calm down anxious humans!"

Joe laughed, and continued his explanation.

"They may not realize it, but regular smokers carefully adjust their nicotine dose by controlling the number of cigarettes they smoke and how deeply and often they inhale. Most use ten or more cigarettes daily and less than five percent smoke fewer than six. Light cigarettes supposedly contain less nicotine but after switching to them from a stronger type, a smoker usually compensates by inhaling more, deeper and more frequently.

"Nicotine is the reason people smoke, Robert. Here's a great example of what I'm talking about. The cigarette butts from restaurant ashtrays in Paris were found to have less tobacco left in them, after tobacco taxes were raised. Since fewer cigarettes were sold, it seems that they were smoked down closer to the filter to squeeze out more nicotine and the last trickle of gooey *goudron*. That's French for tar, Robert."

"Amazing," Robert said.

Silence. Joe lit a cigarette and calmly blew smoke rings at the ceiling. Robert had had enough. He was feeling more than a little bit spooked.

"Joe, when I tell you to wake up, you'll slowly return to your usual self. Wake up, now."

Joe looked at the cigarette in his hand, then around the room and finally at Robert.

"So that's what smoking is all about?" he asked. "It still doesn't make sense to me. Smoking can't be as simple as nicotine addiction. Look at this cigarette here, for example. I don't remember lighting it."

"Your smoking could be very automatic sometimes, Joe, in response to stressful situations. It's not uncommon for heavy smokers to find a cigarette in their hand and not be sure how it got there. Do you remember being a researcher, discovering the reward center in the rat's brain?"

"Yes, that's right," Joe said. "I might have heard about that somewhere before. Strange…" he paused. "I feel as though I've gotten a load off my chest." Robert waited for him to say something more.

Joe looked down and noticed the assignment still lying on the table between them. "I sure was frustrated when I wrote that," he said.

"I guess so, Joe. You seem okay now."

"Yeah. Thanks, Doc. You know, I'm never sure how these sessions are going to turn out. I'm more relaxed than when I arrived today, though."

"This one turned out pretty well then, I'd say" Robert

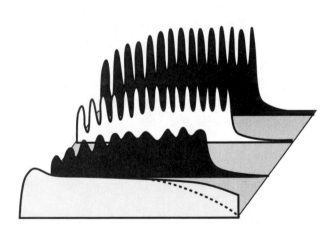

commented. "Are you ready for your next assignment?"

"Sure."

Robert passed Joe a sheet of paper with an unlabelled graph on it.

"See what you can make of this," he instructed.

"What the heck?" asked Joe after studying it briefly. "It looks like a row of aging porcupines or something."

Robert laughed.

"Close," he said. "You wouldn't really want to get tangled up with this thing."

Joe peered at the diagram again, evidently intrigued.

"How about one more clue?" he asked.

"Sure," Robert said. He took a clean sheet of paper from his desk and sketched a quick diagram. "Recognize this?" he asked.

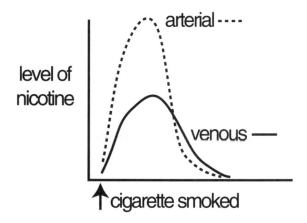

"I do," Joe said. "That's an interesting graph."

"And do you know why it shows more nicotine in the arteries than in the veins?"

"I suppose inhaled nicotine is absorbed in the lungs, and

then passes in high concentration through the arteries to the brain and the rest of the body," said Joe. "The venous blood returning to the heart and lungs, on the other hand, is downstream from the brain and other tissues and the nicotine will have been diluted, absorbed, and broken down by the time it's measured."

"Exactly," said Robert, impressed with Joe's knowledge. "There's your clue."

Their session was over, and Joe left.

* * * * *

Robert made his usual entry in the chart:

Under hypnosis today, Joe surprised me by revealing an in-depth knowledge of nicotine. He seemed to benefit a great deal from today's session, emotionally. I wonder if there's any connection. This is certainly a time of transition for him. He's probably thinking hard about stopping smoking.

Next week we'll discuss nicotine replacement. I'm curious how he'll react to that subject, without hypnosis. It will be a good sign if he shows much interest.

There's been no more news about his cancer.

Joe's assignment for next week: interpret a graph of nicotine delivery systems.

5

Weaning the Monkey

There is little doubt that if it were not for the nicotine in tobacco smoke, people would be little more inclined to smoke than they are to blow bubbles or to light sparklers.

– M.A.H. Russell

(*Author's note:* Nicotine replacement is permitted everywhere, except...)

January 27th

" THERE MUST BE MORE TO SMOKING than nico-
  tine," Joe insisted, shortly into their next session. "I've
been watching how I smoke, and I don't always light up in a
fit of nicotine withdrawal. There's the casual cigarette, the
relaxing one, the cigarette lit to concentrate on a difficult
task, the cigarette to cool down a frustration...."

"That's right," Robert said. "Nicotine withdrawal symptoms only last for two or three weeks at the most. Yet many
ex-smokers still experience occasional cravings for a cigarette, years after quitting. What do you make of it?"

"There must be psychological cravings which outlast the
physical ones," Joe said. "I guess that means nicotine patches and gum don't work in the long run, then."

Joe knew a great deal about nicotine in tobacco smoke,
but was evidently less familiar with nicotine replacement.
Robert set him straight.

"Nicotine replacement definitely works when used properly. Of 100 people who stop smoking cold turkey, about 85
will be smoking regularly again within one year. But studies
have shown that when the patch or gum is used, the success
rate is almost doubled."

Joe thought for a few moments.

"But that still leaves 70 out of 100 quitters smoking again
after one year, doesn't it?"

"You're absolutely right. Of course that also means that
30 people stay quit, instead of just 15. Nicotine replacement
doesn't guarantee success, but it sure helps."

"So the patch or nicotine gum is the secret to quitting successfully?" Joe asked. "If there was an easy, sure-fire way,
even I might consider it."

Robert laughed, gratified that his client was at least now joking about himself.

"Joe, you know there's no simple way out," he said. "Nicotine replacement is just part of the picture. Those who've tried and found quitting too difficult should prepare carefully before trying again. They'd be wise to find some effective ways of coping with stress. It's important for them to get support from other people and to avoid temptation."

"That's easier said than done, Robert. Some days I'd say I feel tempted to smoke every ten minutes."

"Let's see, Joe. That'd be six every hour, about sixteen waking hours... I make that 100 temptations a day. Congratulations, you must be resisting most of them."

"Gee thanks, I think," said Joe.

"Seriously. I suggest that you start keeping track of your smoking, so you can figure out what really triggers you to light up. After you quit, you'll need to avoid or change those situations for awhile. Here, take this and have a look at it later." Robert handed Joe a plastic-laminated index card.

IDENTIFYING HIDDEN TRIGGERS

To identify hidden triggers, mark off four columns on a piece of paper with headings reading *time, place, activity*, and *mood*.

Wrap this record around your cigarette package with an elastic band, and make an entry in each column every time you light up. (If you must leave a building or other situation to smoke, then record what was happening when you first felt the urge.)

After having smoked for about ten days or two hundred cigarettes, look back over the record you have created. The most common entries are your personal triggers.

Next, make plans to avoid or change them.

Joe eagerly accepted the card and read it immediately anyway. Unusual behavior for somebody who really wants to keep smoking, Robert thought.

"I get it," Joe said. "Thanks. But I see one big problem with this approach."

"What's that?"

"If I'm always anxious," Joe said, "then I'll record that I'm anxious every time I smoke. It might look as though anxiety were making me smoke, even if that wasn't true." He handed the card back to Robert.

"I see what you mean." Robert thought for a while. "I know. What about also making an entry on the record every waking hour, even if you don't happen to be smoking at the time? That way you'd get an idea of the times, places, activities, and moods associated with *not* smoking."

"Much better," Joe said. "I'll try that."

"Excellent," said Robert. Joe was really showing signs of interest, and change. "Now, did you give some thought to the graph I gave you last week?"

"Of course I did, Robert. Here it is," said Joe, rummaging in his briefcase and producing the diagram. "I believe it shows the difference between smoking cigarettes and using nicotine patches, gum, and a newly-developed nasal spray. The systems deliver the drug at different rates."

"Exactly," said Robert, providing another copy of the diagram with the labels shown. "The nicotine levels also vary a bit more with cigarettes and nasal spray than with either patches or gum. Why do you think that's important?"

Joe claimed he wasn't sure, so Robert produced a small tape recorder from his desk and set it on the table.

"Listen to this assignment from one of my former clients, Joe. She makes an important point about how nicotine is delivered to the body."

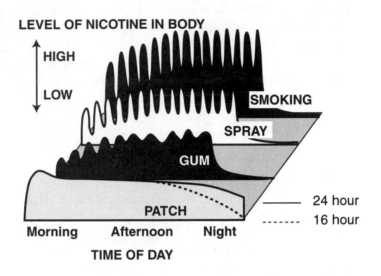

LEVEL OF NICOTINE IN BODY

HIGH

LOW

SMOKING

SPRAY

GUM

PATCH

——— 24 hour
------- 16 hour

Morning   Afternoon   Night

TIME OF DAY

With that Robert punched the "start" button and they settled back to hear the tale.

The Smoker's Cup

A man traveling alone through a desert had the misfortune to meet some bandits who stole all his belongings. In exchange the leader tossed him an elegantly-crafted cup. "Drink to the end of your thirst!" he cried out, before galloping away on his camel.

The poor man was astonished to discover that the cup was always full of water, no matter how much he drank from it. As he struggled on through the stressful heat he came to cherish the magical treasure. The first draught in the cool of morning was just as exquisite as one drawn in the blistering hell of mid-day.

One night he had a vivid and terrifying dream, in which an angel warned him that the cup was the devil's trap: each drink would cost him five minutes of his life!

The poor man was filled with fear, but couldn't resist satisfying his thirst. The cup seemed to be his only means of survival and he simply couldn't bring himself to throw it away.

After several days of this anguish the angel reappeared in his dreams to offer him relief, telling him that he'd never be thirsty if he simply wore a water-patch on his arm. "But," the angel warned "you will always have to carry the cup with you."

At first the traveler found that the patch provided him all the water he needed. Then thoughts of drinking from the cup again began to trouble him. He was never actually thirsty, but he missed the smooth satisfaction of a cool drink.

"Perhaps just one sip?" he kept wondering The obsession became a torment worse than the heat that scorched his throat with every breath.

The temptation proved to be too strong for the unfortunate fellow. In the hottest hour of a very hot day, when the sun was high in the sky, he sipped from the seductive cup once again.

The next day he had a sip to wake up with, and one at each meal. He resumed drinking regularly from the cup, about 20 times a day. "It's not so bad," he told himself. "After all, I can stop anytime I want to."

The poor fellow died at 42 of heart and lung disease. The cup was a problem, but he would have lived to 65 if only he had managed to find the satisfying solution inside himself.

The recording ended there.

"Do you get it?" Robert asked.

"I think so. She's saying that the faster a rewarding drug

is delivered to the body, the more addictive it's likely to be. The poor fellow got more satisfaction from feeling thirsty and then drinking, than from never feeling thirsty."

"That right. A high concentration of nicotine 'spikes' the brain just seven seconds after a few puffs on a cigarette. It takes several minutes for nicotine to be slowly released from the gum though, and the patch yields a steady level all day. Let's look at that graph again."

Joe pointed out the rapid rises of the "nasal spray" line.

"So does that mean the spray is addictive?" he asked.

Robert pondered that question for a few moments. "I wouldn't call it addictive in the same way that smoking is," he said, "but in one study using nicotine nasal spray 43% of the ex-smokers continued to use the product one year after their last cigarette. What's more, their average nicotine blood-levels at the end of the smoke-free year were about 80% of their pre-quitting value."

Joe said nothing. Robert reached for some papers on his desk. "Perhaps it would be easier to look at the four nicotine delivery systems separately," he said. "Here's the spray, which produces quite a rapid rise of blood nicotine levels."

"It seems that speedier delivery makes the product more attractive," Joe said. "That's basic fast food philosophy."

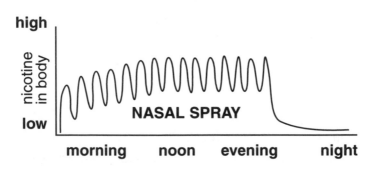

"Precisely," said Robert with a smile. "That may partly explain why smoking is so addictive, but why nobody expresses much interest in using nicotine patches beyond a few months after quitting. They just provide a smooth, steady supply of nicotine throughout the day."

"I see. And what about nicotine gum?" Joe asked.

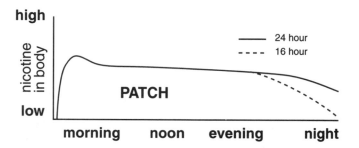

"It fits somewhere between the patch and the spray, in terms of the way it delivers nicotine. When used properly, nicotine gum provides a steady supply of nicotine that can be controlled by the ex-smoker. It's interesting that in one study of nicotine gum, 25% of the ex-smokers were still using it one year after they quit, and 12.5% were still using it two years after quitting. It obviously works for some people in the long run."

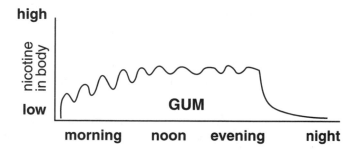

"Well, that makes sense," Joe concluded. "The quicker nicotine is delivered, and the more that delivery is under the user's control, the more habit-forming the system will be."

"Right, Joe. Of course the cigarette is the most addictive way to deliver nicotine, by far, because it can provide such a large dose of the drug on demand so quickly. So…"

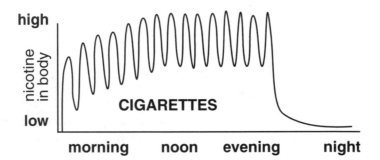

There was a pause in their conversation. Robert's unspoken conclusion was that since cigarettes are addictive, they should be better controlled in order to limit the damage done.

Joe cleared his throat before speaking. He now seemed more interested in reasons *not* to use nicotine replacement. "Isn't nicotine replacement dangerous, though?" he asked. "I've heard of people dying while using nicotine patches, maybe because they smoked at the same time."

Robert was quick to reassure him.

"Smoking while using the patch can give the body a bigger jolt of nicotine than it has ever experienced, and that's not a very good idea at all," he said. "But nicotine replacement is extremely safe when used as directed. And of course you have to dispose of used patches properly, where kids or pets won't get at them."

"Okay," said Joe. "But it seems to me that nicotine replacement itself could be addictive. I certainly wouldn't want to get hooked," he added with an ironic smile.

"Don't worry about that, Joe. The bottom line is that nicotine replacement definitely helps a smoker to quit. The nasal spray and gum may be slightly habit-forming for some people, but that's nothing compared to smoking. You, my friend, might benefit from using a patch or gum someday."

"Are you *sure* nicotine itself isn't harmful?" Robert's reluctant patient inquired.

"Nicotine doesn't cause the death and sickness from smoking," Robert emphasized. "The real culprits are the by-products of burning tobacco. Over 4,000 chemicals besides nicotine have been identified in cigarette smoke, at least 43 of which cause cancer. Tobacco smoke also contains potent poisons such as arsenic, cadmium, and carbon monoxide."

Joe seemed to stiffen a bit at the specifics, before Robert continued with his explanation.

"Although it can be addictive when smoked, nicotine alone isn't particularly harmful if used in moderation. It raises the heart rate and blood pressure and that might create problems for somebody with heart disease, but for healthy people it's essentially harmless when used sensibly in reasonable doses."

"Problems?" Joe asked. "You mean heart attacks?"

"No, but it's wise to check with a physician before using any kind of nicotine replacement if you have any doubts about your health. Don't forget, cigarettes usually provide far more nicotine than any form of replacement does, and a bunch of poisons and carcinogens besides."

Joe abruptly changed the topic. "How's a person supposed to use nicotine replacement, anyway?"

"It's easy, Joe. The spray would simply go up your nose. Not too often, mind you. The patch is applied daily to some clean non-hairy skin. Nicotine 'gum' may need some explanation, because it's useless to treat it like regular gum and swallow the juice."

"Really?" Joe asked. "Why is that?"

"Because of the way blood flows through the body, nicotine absorbed from the stomach goes directly to the liver where it is metabolized, or broken down. So the brain does not get very much nicotine, in that case. On the other hand most of the nicotine entering the body any other way will reach those empty receptors in the nicotine-starved brain."

"That makes sense. So a fellow just needs to chew on the gum and not swallow?"

"Not exactly. Here, take this and read it over," Robert said, handing Joe a wallet-sized instruction card.

THE CORRECT WAY TO USE NICOTINE GUM

Chew a piece briefly and then park it in one cheek. You should feel a tingling inside your cheek, and a peppery taste in your mouth.

After a few minutes, chew the product a few times and move it over into the other cheek. Repeat this every few minutes.

Fresh pieces of gum should be used regularly throughout the day.

Don't drink anything before or while using the gum, especially acidic juices like orange and grapefruit.

Joe read the card carefully.

"But why shouldn't a person drink or eat anything while using the gum?" he asked. Robert explained that nicotine only crosses the skin inside the mouth when in a slightly alkaline state, and that any acidity such as a trace of orange juice can prevent the proper absorption.

"Right, I get it," Joe said. "Much the same thing applies to cigar and pipe smoke."

Now it was Robert's turn to ask for an explanation. "Tell me about that, Joe. You're the smoke expert. So it's not a good idea to smoke a cigar or pipe while using the gum?"

Joe laughed. "Of course not, Robert. That would defeat the whole purpose. Cigars and pipes cause oral cancer and other diseases. What I'm saying is that they produce an alkaline smoke and so the nicotine from them can be absorbed through the skin inside the mouth."

"Isn't that true of cigarettes, too?" Robert asked, testing the unfamiliar waters they were sailing into, blown along by the winds of change. Joe looked quizzically at Robert, hesitating somewhat before responding.

"Cigarettes used to be harsh and alkaline, too, but modern manufacturers use certain types of tobacco, curing processes, and additives to produce a neutral smoke. It goes down more easily, and the nicotine can then be absorbed from the lungs. We're making huge sales in countries where the competition doesn't have our, um, technology."

Joe frowned, and asked "Robert, what should I do?"

"That depends on your preference, Joe. Some people prefer the patch for its convenience and predictability. Others like the gum because it gets something in their mouth instead of a cigarette. Of course, one could always chew on a toothpick or something. There's been some research about using both patch and gum together, but that's not official."

"No, that's not what I meant," Joe said. Robert then very deliberately interrupted before he could say anything more. Above all, he didn't want to be put in the position of giving advice; the decisions were all Joe's. They both knew it.

"What should you do? My friend, nicotine replacement is only part of the overall solution to smoking. It's not a 'magic bullet' that miraculously ends a person's habit for them. I think one also has to change perspective a bit, and perhaps alter one's environment. Recent ex-smokers might want to try thinking something like 'that poor fool' rather than 'I wish I could have one' when they see somebody smoking."

"Right," said Joe, nodding his head and grinning slightly. "I think I get what you're saying. It isn't easy thing to change perspective, though. Old habits die hard."

"But like us, Joe, once they die, they're gone forever."

"Right again, Robert. Right again. About the old habits, that is. But I've been wondering about death. Do you believe in heaven or hell or an afterlife of some kind?"

"I'm not certain what comes next," Robert said, evading the question, "but I believe there's a bit of both heaven and hell right here and now on this planet. Everything we do or don't do contributes to the situation."

Joe stopped asking questions. He got up and wandered over to the window. Some children were playing in the fresh-ly fallen snow, making imprints of "angels" by lying on their backs and sweeping their arms up and down. He muttered something that could have been "Lord help us all."

"I've really got to go now," Joe said, returning from his reverie. "I have things to do."

After arranging to meet again in one week, Joe abruptly took his leave.

* * * * *

Robert opened Joe's chart and wrote a short note:

Joe isn't quite ready to quit yet, but he's making progress. I could tell that we got to the point today because Joe started asking for advice.

He must come to his own conclusions. And he will.

6

Delay Death, Avoid Taxes

Our remedies oft in ourselves lie,
which we ascribe to heaven.
— Shakespeare

February 3rd

"WHAT DO YOU THINK, ROBERT? Maybe I should just take off somewhere and die," Joe said at the beginning of their next meeting.

The pathologists still hadn't been able to identify his cancer. The surgeons were reluctant to operate, for fear of spreading the disease throughout his body. The team had decided to try radiation therapy, hoping to shrink the tumor or at least slow its growth.

Something effective was needed to turn Joe's down mood around. He looked worn out and disinterested.

"I'm sorry to hear things aren't going better," said Robert.

Joe waved off the sympathy with a dismissive gesture of his hand. He was tough, and a bit frightened.

"Forget it, he said. "What's up for today?"

Robert took a deep breath, and a bit of a risk. Perhaps it was time to show Joe the big carrot: the benefits of quitting.

"You probably don't realize it Joe, but smoking is actually good for you," he said then quickly added "sort of."

Joe tilted his head to one side and raised his eyebrows.

"I've discovered a major benefit of smoking," Robert continued, "and I'd like you to tell me what you think of it."

Joe looked intently at Robert for a few seconds, as if weighing an important decision. He saw no malice in the other's eyes, and smiled. What could Robert have up his sleeve now?

"Without hearing anything more about it," he said "I think it's nonsense."

"But you'll give it a listen anyway?" asked Robert.

"Sure, just to humor you though."

"Great," Robert said. "First of all, I have to tell you that my cat Max deserves some of the credit for this scientific breakthrough. His part in our amazing discovery was as accidental as mine. I brewed up some strong coffee as usual before sitting down to a computer-review of the healthy effects of smoking. Some of what I found was quite interesting, by the way."

Joe relaxed as Robert entertained and educated him.

"One recent editorial entitled *The Benefits of Smoking?* seemed promising at first." Robert continued, "The writer suggested that it's foolish to deny the benefits of smoking, for certain groups. She noted that smoking helps some people relate to one another, eases tensions, allows one to take some time for oneself, controls appetite, and is a source of pleasure. So it's not all bad."

"That's right," Joe said. "Smokers are completely misunderstood. You rarely hear the benefits of smoking mentioned anymore. It's not like the good old days when doctors actually recommended certain brands."

Robert heartily agreed, and immediately proposed that they discuss the benefits of smoking.

"The gratification familiar to any smoker is felt immediately, but the disastrous consequences are delayed for years. If it were the other way around, do you think that anybody would smoke?"

"What do you mean, Robert? You mean if smoking produced an instant heart attack?"

"Something like that. You smoke but instead of pleasure you experience a few minutes of severe shortness of breath. Nothing but extra oxygen can relieve it. Or maybe a cigarette produces the immediate chest pain of angina, or a disabling stroke. You can't speak or move properly, perhaps forever. Nothing fatal, of course. About fifteen or twenty years later you'd experience a mild calming effect. Who'd smoke, if the sequence of pleasurable and painful effects was reversed, or even if they all happened at once?"

Joe smiled softly, not missing the point. He chuckled before reminding Robert that he was supposed to be explaining how Max and he discovered the mysterious major benefit of smoking.

"Oh yes," Robert continued. "Things were looking pretty bleak for the article I intended to write about The Health Benefits of Smoking. After searching a few thousand more medical references I unearthed some fascinating trivia. For example it seems the early Egyptians used tobacco to preserve their pharaohs. Apparently scientists investigating the ancient mummy of Ramses II were startled to find his body cavities stuffed with tobacco. Before this discovery, people believed that tobacco was unknown outside America until Columbus's time. Oh, and there are some suggestions that smoking might be slightly beneficial for ulcerative colitis, hypertension of pregnancy, uterine cancer, and perhaps for Parkinson's disease."

"Get to the point, man," said Joe good-naturedly.

"Well, we tell kids not to say anything if they haven't anything good to say. I began to wonder how my editor would feel about receiving a two-paragraph article. This was truly my darkest creative hour.

"I must be one of the luckiest humans alive, Joe. Just as I was about to give up hope Max leapt up and danced a very fancy feline jig on the computer keyboard. My coffee slopped all over the machine. I rapidly dispatched the delinquent beast back to the floor, but I feared the worst. Have you ever lost several hours of unsaved computer-work forever into deep cyberspace, Joe?

"That's bad." Joe gravely agreed. "Once is once too often. So then what happened?"

"Mysterious symbols flashed onto the screen. The computer whirred and buzzed alarmingly for what seemed like an eternity. To my utter astonishment the compu-seizure ended with the ultimate health benefit of smoking displayed on the screen, complete with a long list of references. Imagine discovering by coffee-catastrophe a medical fact with the potential to save literally millions of lives, and endless misery and suffering! Are you ready for it, Joe? *Smokers live longer and much healthier lives after quitting!*"

Joe wasn't very enthusiastic about the amazing discovery.

"I don't believe that smokers have that much to gain by quitting," he said with folded arms.

"But they certainly do, Joe. You're not alone in having a hard time accepting this. I don't have a more recent figure at hand, but in 1990 about a third of all smokers in the United States either didn't believe that smoking was harmful, or that quitting would reduce the risk. They were mistaken, of course. Stopping smoking is usually the best thing anyone can do for their health."

"Okay, but what *exactly* are the supposed benefits?"

"They are quite impressive, and in some instances almost immediate. Here, have a reminder card for later." Robert handed Joe another card, and waited while he read it.

> ## *Some of the benefits of stopping smoking*
> - Within a few weeks of quitting the chance of a sudden heart attack is decreased, and the cough of chronic bronchitis often clears up.
> - After fifteen years the ex-smoker's chance of developing cancer or having a stroke is about equal to that of somebody who has never smoked (These benefits apply both to 'healthy' smokers and those who already have smoking-related disease).
> - Women who stop smoking in the first three months of their pregnancy run the same risk of having a low-birthweight baby as do women who've never smoked.

"And check out this graph, Joe," Robert said, producing a chart from his desk. "It shows how the risk of death is reduced after quitting. A male 45-year-old pack-a-day smoker stands a 22% chance of dying before reaching the age of 62. That risk of dying within the next 17 years can be reduced to just 11% by starting to live smoke-free again, beginning at age 45."

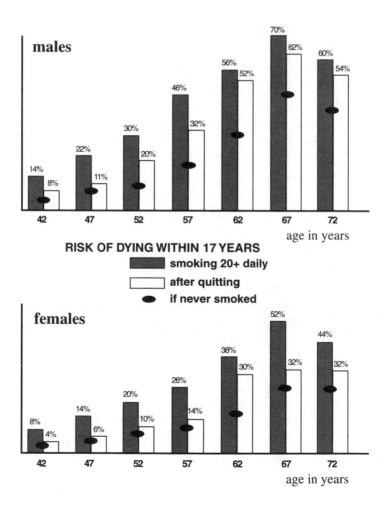

"How's that?" Joe was clearly interested now, leaning forward in his chair.

"Here, I'll show you. One of these graphs is for males, and one is for females. First, find the pair of bars corresponding to your age, shown across the bottom of the graph. The grey bar on the left of each pair shows your risk of dying within 17 years if you smoke 20 or more cigarettes daily.

"Suppose you quit, and stay smoke-free. Your risk then decreases to that shown by the lighter-colored bar on the right of the pair." Joe inspected the graph.

"You mean my risk would decrease from 22% to 11%?" he asked. "Where did you get this?"

"I drew this up based on data from the United States Department of Health and Human Services document entitled *The Health Benefits of Smoking Cessation, A Report of the Surgeon General*," Robert said.

"But what about me?" Joe asked. "I've already got cancer from smoking." That was the first time he'd made any direct reference to a connection between smoking and his cancer.

"These kinds of benefits are *only* available to smokers who quit," Robert said. "If you don't, you remain at high risk. Whatever state you're in, you can enjoy the rest of your life more by quitting smoking.

"Of course, people who've never smoked have little room for improvement," he added. Joe looked skeptically at Robert as he realized how ridiculous that last statement was.

"You're just saying the benefit of repeatedly hitting your head on a wall is that it feels good to stop," Joe said.

Robert didn't say anything.

"Really, do you think if I stop smoking I will... live... longer," Joe said slowly, as if shifting from just knowing certain facts, to understanding them.

"There are no guarantees Joe, but you'll probably find a smoke-free life more enjoyable, and perhaps live longer."

Joe looked at the graph again.

"Your logic is impeccable but I don't think you and Max are going to win any Nobel Prize," he said.

"I'm afraid you're right," Robert conceded, "but at least we get to share it with you." He noticed Joe's thoughtful expression. "Look, I hope I haven't confused you today. I really want you to have this information, and I'm just trying to make it easier to take."

"No problem, Robert. I appreciate the, umm, attempt at humor. Keep your day job, though."

"Sure thing. Here, have this," Robert said, passing Joe a pamphlet. "Just to make sure there's no misunderstanding, here's a listing of the major conclusions of the U.S. Surgeon General's 1990 report on the benefits of quitting smoking."

Joe slipped both the pamphlet and the graph into his attache case before he spoke.

"It's crazy, but I knew that smoking was harmful and there was some point to quitting, but I never considered the figures. I never thought they applied to me. I'm not sure where this leaves me, but thanks anyway. I mean it."

"You're welcome, Joe. You might also be interested in this older paper about smoking and injuries." Robert passed him the article. Joe stood and walked over to the window, and scanned the few pages.

"Smoking is the leading cause of fire death and the second leading cause of fire-related injury in the United States," he read. "About 4% of house fires are caused by children playing with matches, cigarette lighters, or other smoking materials... An estimated 14% of burn hospitalizations are cigarette-related... Compared with non-smokers, smokers may have a 50% increased risk for motor vehicle accidents, especially at night… cigarette smokers appear twice as likely as non-smokers to be injured at work… male infantry trainees who smoked had 1.7 times more lower extremity injuries than non-smokers."

Joe paused. "I can buy the house-fire thing," he said, "but why on earth would smokers have more traffic accidents? And more injuries?"

"Get a bit drowsy from carbon monoxide poisoning?" Robert responded. "Drop a cigarette in your lap while driving? Delayed healing due to poor circulation?"

"I'm not so sure," said Joe.

"Well, Joe, I'd like to see any research to suggest that smokers have fewer injuries, less traffic accidents, fewer house fires, faster wound healing, and so on. The bottom line is that there are many benefits to quitting, including sparing the people around you from the indirect consequences of your smoking."

Joe thought about that.

"Are you trying to make me feel guilty?" he asked.

"No," Robert responded. "I'm not even trying."

Joe laughed. "Well I do!" He turned and looked out the window, as he'd done near the end of their last meeting. It was as though he was looking for something.

Robert's office was on the second floor of an older renovated house. Large trees lined the quiet street, branches bare for the winter moment. Joe thought back over the years and the seasons of his life. It was definitely too soon to die, he thought. There was much he had to do.

"It's odd," Joe finally said. "I've smoked all my life, but it seems I've never really thought about it. Not really thought about it."

About a minute or so passed without a word.

"I think that's enough for today," Robert said.

Sometimes they'd talk for twenty minutes or so, sometimes half an hour. They usually both sensed when it was time to end. It had been another short but useful session, and Joe had taken a huge step forward.

* * * * *

In a somber mood after Joe's departure, Robert wrote his thoughts in the clinical record:

Joe is taking stock of the situation. He's well into the contemplation stage now, seriously considering change. With any luck he'll very soon turn the corner and make a commitment to quit.

I feel sorry for Joe. It's sad to see him realizing what he's missing out on by smoking.

At this point I want to help Joe build up his reasons to change his behavior. He doesn't seem terribly afraid of dying. Perhaps considering the effect of his actions on others will motivate him to quit smoking, at least.

I always find this stage a bit frustrating, because the commitment to stop smoking seems so close but hasn't been reached yet. Still, I've come a long way from when I used to "threaten" smokers with the dangers of smoking.

Next week: We'll have to talk about children and smoking.

A Few Benefits of Stopping Smoking

1. Quitting smoking has major and immediate health benefits for men and women of all ages. Benefits apply to persons with and without diseases related to smoking.
2. Former smokers live longer than continuing smokers. For example, persons who quit smoking before age 50 have one-half the risk of dying in the next 15 years compared with those who continue to smoke.
3. Smoking cessation decreases the risk of lung and other cancers, heart attack, stroke, and chronic lung disease (such as emphysema).
4. Women who stop smoking before pregnancy or during the first 3 to 4 months of pregnancy reduce their risk of having a low birthweight baby to that of women who never smoked.
5. The health benefits of smoking cessation far exceed any risks from any moderate weight gain, or any adverse psychological effects that may follow quitting.

7

Kids Can Smoke, Too

People have many different kinds of pleasure. The real one is the one for which they will forsake all others.

— Proust

February 10th

JOE SHOWED UP A BIT EARLY the next week and waited patiently in the small reception area. Robert arrived shortly afterwards. As usual they first caught up on news both good and bad.

The bad news, from Joe's perspective, was that he'd been summoned to an upcoming government hearing on tobacco control. The thought of testimony under oath made his heart race as though he'd just chain-smoked an entire pack of *Slayer's* Fill-Tar-Tip King Size Cancer Sticks.

On a much more positive note the radiation treatments were shrinking his cancer.

"You may find this hard to believe," Joe explained, "but they tell me it's a bizarre mutation of a rare tumor which only affects camels living in a certain part of the Sahara desert." Indeed, Robert wasn't sure what to make of that, at all.

"They figure I picked it up there many years ago when a camel licked my face. My cheek broke out in a rash for a few days but then it went away and I never thought about it again. Until Dr. Billmore asked, that is."

"Really?" Robert asked. "That seems quite incredible." But was it any more unbelievable than Mad Cow disease? It was getting harder and harder to keep up with medical discoveries and advances these days, he thought. What an unusual case.

"Yeah, it was kind of freakish how they made the connection. Dr. Billmore fell asleep at his desk with his head down on an ancient National Geographic magazine, and woke up with a picture of a camel imprinted on his face!"

Robert was growing very suspicious. This was definitely some kind of joke. What an extraordinary way to handle a cancer diagnosis, even if it was responding to treatment.

"So then he went to discuss my case with a colleague. They had a good laugh at the camel-face. Dr. Billmore said he'd never had a zoonose before."

(A *zoonose* is a disease transmitted from animal to man, and Robert groaned at the pun.) Joe continued his story.

"The other fellow suddenly remembered a question about zoonoses from his final exam in medical school, and wondered aloud if my problem wasn't something of the sort. After learning about the camel incident they ran some more tests on my cancer, and traced it back to the camel's lick."

"You must be kidding," said Robert. "This is the first case of a 'dromedoma' I've ever heard of."

Joe explained that the tumor had actually responded so well to the radiation treatment that the surgeons were now prepared to operate. What's more, there didn't appear to have been any spread to the rest of his body.

"That's fantastic!" Robert exclaimed, jumping to his feet and grabbing Joe's hand. He shook it vigourously. "That's really great news."

Joe's surgeons were apparently getting quite excited about cutting the tumor out for him, once the radiation treatments were finished. "They're probably sharpening their knives for me right now," he joked.

After his spontaneous celebration of the good news Robert experienced an unsettling afterthought: Did this mean that Joe was going to survive, keep on smoking, and carry on his work? Much as he'd tried to to keep the man's profession and his problems separate in his mind, Robert had thought more than once of the the ironic justice involved in a tobacco industry leader developing a cancer.

He was being watched. Joe had stopped smiling and was watching him think. What now?

"Robin must be so relieved," said Robert. "And just in

time for Valentine's Day. Do you two have any plans?"

"You bet," said Joe smoothly. "We're going on a road trip, just like we used to do. We'd get in the car and just disappear for a few days. I have to be at a shareholders' meeting here next Monday, but we plan to have no plans for two days."

Robert recalled that Robin had been somewhat dissatisfied with her life before quitting smoking. "How are you two getting along, by the way?" he asked.

"Very well, these days. This cancer thing has helped us appreciate each other more. She hasn't been harassing me about my smoking, either. She just says she's sure I'll do the best I can."

"That's great. Are you taking the kids on the road trip?" Ben would be about nine years old now and Mary eleven, Robert figured.

"Not this time!" said Joe. "I love 'em, but Robin and I need time alone together from time to time. Besides, the ungrateful little wretches are always on my case about smoking." Joe smiled broadly as he lit a cigarette.

The smoke rose to vanish into the ventilated corners of the ceiling. A cloud passed over Joe's expression and he looked down at the cigarette in his hand.

"These things really aren't good for kids, are they?" he asked. "That's what the Environmental Protection Agency says, anyway."

Robert said nothing, waiting. Joe got up and wandered over to the window as he recited some facts and figures he'd long since committed to memory:

"Between 150,000 and 300,000 cases of bronchitis and pneumonia annually in American children below the age of eighteen months, resulting in 7,500 to 15,000 hospitalizations. Fluid collections in children's middle ears, possibly leading to infections. In asthmatic children, more frequent and more severe symptoms. New cases of asthma, probably."

Joe paused to turn and look expectantly at Robert. What did he want, or need?

"You're absolutely right, Joe," Robert said very carefully, "The big deal about smoking around kids is that it makes them sick, stunts their growth, and sometimes kills them. Even if kids don't pick up the smoking habit from their parents, they are affected by tobacco smoke."

Joe took a deep haul from his cigarette. The corners of his mouth pulled back in a half-grimace, and then he let a thick stream of smoke slowly escape. Robert and he watched it rise and dissipate.

"Second-hand smoke" Joe said, returning to his chair. "Sidestream smoke, ETS, environmental tobacco smoke, call it what you want. Very controversial recently. No-smoking bylaws and that sort of thing. Tell me, what do you think of it, Robert?"

"A smoke-filled room is surprisingly dangerous in the long run," Robert said. "The tobacco at the tip of a cigarette burns hotter and more completely when air is drawn through it. The 'sidestream' smoke coming off the smoldering tip contains more incompletely-burned compounds. It's probably more carcinogenic."

Their gazes converged on the thin gray column rising from the glowing end of Joe's cigarette as he held it out between them. Eight inches up, the smoke broke into a turbulent cloud before dispersing.

"You'd think that a few whiffs of smoke wouldn't amount to much," Joe commented.

"You might not think so, but I've seen asthmatic children in hospital suffer after visits from their smoking parents. The stuff clings to their clothes, and the kids are allergic to it."

Robert shifted in his seat, and his voice betrayed his

impatience. "All they'd have to do is hang a coat and hat outside the house somewhere, and wear them only when smoking. They just have to leave the hat and coat outside, and wash their hands and face upon returning to the house. That's all. Nobody is asking them to stop smoking."

"You take that issue pretty seriously, Robert," said Joe.

"I do. There must be *no smoking at all* around asthmatic children. It can kill them. I've seen it happen. Bans on smoking in public places and advice not to smoke around children aren't just the latest fashion in thought control," Robert insisted. "They can prevent disease and death."

"Is there really any good proof that secondhand smoke is harmful to healthy people though?" Joe asked.

Robert was quick to respond.

"Healthy adult non-smokers who live with regular smokers are 1.3 times more likely to have a heart attack, or to develop angina or lung cancer, compared with those breathing clean air. Here, I've got a recent review article about the overall effects of tobacco smoke on kids." Robert quickly dug into his files to find it, then read from the summary. "Every year, among American children, tobacco is associated with an estimated 284 to 360 deaths from lower respiratory tract illnesses and fires started by smoking, 354,000 to 2.2 million ear infections, somewhere between 5,200 and 165,000 operations to put tubes in kids' ears, 14,000 to 21,000 operations to remove their tonsils and/or adenoids, 529,000 visits to the doctor because of asthma, 1.3 to 2 million visits for coughs, and in children under the age of 5 years, 260,000 to 436,000 episodes of bronchitis and somewhere between 115,000 and 190,000 episodes of pneumonia."

"Would you like a copy of the report?" Robert asked.

"No, that's okay," Joe said, placing his cigarette in the ashtray. *And smoking around an infant or during pregnancy increases the risk of sudden infant death*, he thought.

"You must think I'm nuts," said Joe. "Sometimes I think I am, too. But tobacco's been my life, my career so far."

He paused for air.

"It's also cost me dearly. Robin smoked through all three of her pregnancies, and after Joey was born." Joe hesitated, and blinked.

Robert reached out and rested a sympathetic hand on his shoulder. "You're not to blame for that, or for not knowing any better."

Smoking during pregnancy or around a baby increases the chance of having it die from sudden infant death syndrome (SIDS). Smoking during pregnancy also makes a baby about half a pound shy of normal birthweight, and increases the chances of that baby dying at or shortly after birth.

In the United States annually, tobacco use is responsible for an estimated 19,000 to 141,000 abortions, 32,000-61,000 low-birthweight infants, and 14,000-26,000 newborns requiring intensive care. It also accounts for 1,900 to 4,800 infant deaths from birthing complications, and 1,200 to 2,200 deaths from SIDS.

"Thanks," said Joe. "but perhaps I *should* have known better. You know, a fellow can only deny something for so long. I might be a fool, but I'm not an innocent fool. I ignored many misgivings in order to advance my career in the tobacco trade."

This was an unusual admission from Joe, one that hinted at extraordinary things to come.

"Let me tell you about a dream I had the other night," Joe continued. "I'm curious how you'll interpret it."

Robert listened closely.

"I was playing on a beautiful tropical beach with my children, kicking a ball around and splashing in the clear warm water. It was a real tropical paradise scene with palm trees, an umbrella for shade, and a little cabana at the edge of the forest. You get the picture.

"I found a gold coin in the sand, and then another. It was incredible. The more I looked, the more I found. I ran around gathering up the treasure, laughing and calling to my family to come and help me.

"The children paid no attention. They played and splashed in the water, carefree. I felt so happy in that dream, until the water began to recede.

"The ocean pulled back to expose a seabed of almost solid gold. I remember fish flopping about, stranded by the retreating waters. And there was a terrible smell. There was something rotten out there, which had previously been hidden.

"Something rose from the horizon like a curtain being drawn up to the sky. I ran to rescue my children, suddenly realizing what was happening. The tidal wave curled over us, impossibly high, about to break down onto the beach.

"That's when I woke up," said Joe. "What do you make of it? Should I sell my beach cabin?"

Robert chuckled and took a few seconds before answering. "Tidal waves are caused by underwater earthquakes, Joe. Somewhere out in that ocean, the earth itself was grinding and shifting. Big changes were happening. What do you think is behind the wave in your dream?"

"I don't know. I hadn't thought of that. I figured maybe it had something to do with money and children, but I see your point. I'll have to think about it."

"Why don't you do that, Joe. And perhaps for your next assignment you could put something together about women and smoking. Next week let's talk about money, since you mentioned it."

Joe pressed Robert for some guidelines on his assignment but it was left open. Whatever he thought was best. "Just put something together about women and smoking," Robert repeated. "And have a Happy Valentine's Day."

After Joe left Robert sat for awhile before making a note in Joe's chart. As he wrote he experienced a deep sadness that settled and clung onto him like stale tobacco smoke. Perhaps it was from thinking about those children.

He trudged home. It was unseasonably warm, and raining to soak the dwindling banks of rotting snow that lined the city's major arteries. A smoke-gray sky had obscured any sun all day. Now the manufactured lights cast long shadows on a miserable winter's evening.

* * * * *

The clinical note for the day:

Fantastic news: Joe's cancer appears to be benign, and can be taken care of. Still, he's far from healthy.

Joe is a different man than the fellow I first met a few weeks ago. Today when we talked about smoking and children he was obviously upset at remembering his dead son. He recounted an interesting dream in which a tidal wave swept over him and his family as they played on a beach of gold. I wonder if he's having further doubts about his involvement with promoting tobacco.

Money is obviously a big motivation for Joe, so next week I'll offer him the chance to make an easy million dollars.

Joe's assignment: a report on women and smoking.

8

Money To Burn?

It is a great piece of skill to know how to guide your luck even while waiting for it.

— Baltasar Gracian

February 17th

THE NEXT WEEK Joe's secretary phoned at the last moment to say that he'd be late. Something had come up. Robert took advantage of the opportunity to write to Joe's doctor.

Dear Dr. Billmore:
                re: Mr. Joseph Hamel

Thanks again for sending me this interesting patient.

Mr. Hamel's situation is somewhat complicated. As you know, he is a public relations and marketing expert who late last year was diagnosed with a rare form of cancer. His past medical history and family history are unremarkable, except for his having smoked at least a pack of cigarettes daily for about thirty years. He is certainly addicted to nicotine.

So far I have concentrated on helping him to understand the consequences of smoking. At first he demonstrated a tremendous resistance to quitting, being an important figurehead in the tobacco industry and a loyal smoker. Lately Joe has made significant progress, seeming closer to making a commitment to change. He has begun to really think about what smoking means. He may also be questioning the part he plays in promoting such an unhealthy product.

Joe might discover a new side to his personality when he quits. After all, he's been using nicotine as a coping strategy throughout his whole maturation process, from adolescence to adulthood. He will have to find other ways to deal with anxiety, fatigue, boredom, and the rest of his smoking 'triggers.'

Many ex-smokers find themselves more irritable,

anxious, depressed and distracted in the first few weeks after quitting. This is normal and is due to the change in brain chemistry that occurs when nicotine is withdrawn. Most ex-smokers gradually return to being their usual selves, smoke-free. Others may never quite get back to the same mood and personality. Instead, they remain anxious and irritable for many months and are more likely to take up smoking again.

I am not sure which pattern Joe will follow. It's very important that he be thoroughly prepared before he attempts to stop smoking. Nevertheless, please use every appropriate opportunity to strongly urge him to stop, while offering unconditional support.

I will keep you posted as to developments. Thank you once again for the opportunity to work with this most interesting fellow.

Sincerely,

Dr. Borenot

Robert had just finished sealing the envelope when a very flustered Joe burst into the office.

"Stockholder's meeting," he explained between flinging his coat onto the rack and collapsing into his chair. "I'm fed up with this whole mess."

Joe lit a cigarette and inhaled deeply.

"So what's up?" Robert asked, after a short silence.

"Profits are up, Robert, but our share prices are down. We have a perfectly legal product, but the anti-smoking lobby has been running a smear campaign and discouraging investment in tobacco. There should be a law against it. Pension plans and mutual funds are starting to sell off our stock."

"Well, it's never too late to get out," Robert suggested. "Quit smoking, quit your job, and save yourself the trouble."

With an impatient scowl Joe inhaled what looked like a half inch of his cigarette. He was in no mood for discussion. A protester had infiltrated the meeting and made a scene before being removed. A stack of well-funded lawsuits had been initiated against the tobacco industry. For the first time, state health insurance schemes were suing to recover the costs of treating smoking-related disease. And Joe wasn't looking forward to testifying at the government hearings.

Robert clasped his hands in front of his chest with his index fingers extended. He leaned his chin onto the support they offered, and closed his eyes. Joe stared at him. Robert looked up then, catching Joe's gaze.

"How would you like to make an easy million dollars?" Robert asked.

"Seriously?" Joe replied. "What's the deal?"

"The annual cost of smoking one pack of cigarettes daily is between $1,000 and $2,000 in Canada, or about $800 in the United States. That's local currency, of course. Two thousand dollars invested at 10% interest tax-free compounded annually for 42 years yields $1,085,231." Robert handed Joe a graph and a sheet of figures.

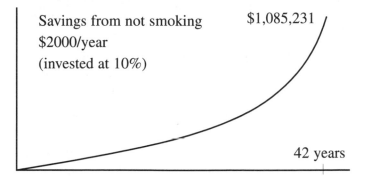

Savings from not smoking $1,085,231
$2000/year
(invested at 10%)

42 years

How money saved by not smoking
will grow when invested at 10%

Year	Annual Savings	Total Saved	Year	Annual Savings	Total Saved
1	$2,000	$2,200	22	$2,000	$144,286
2	$2,000	$4,420	23	$2,000	$160,714
3	$2,000	$6,862	24	$2,000	$178,786
4	$2,000	$9,548	25	$2,000	$198,664
5	$2,000	$12,503	26	$2,000	$220,530
6	$2,000	$15,753	27	$2,000	$244,584
7	$2,000	$19,329	28	$2,000	$271,042
8	$2,000	$23,262	29	$2,000	$300,146
9	$2,000	$27,588	30	$2,000	$332,161
10	$2,000	$32,346	31	$2,000	$367,377
11	$2,000	$37,581	32	$2,000	$406,114
12	$2,000	$43,339	33	$2,000	$448,726
13	$2,000	$49,673	34	$2,000	$495,598
14	$2,000	$56,640	35	$2,000	$547,158
15	$2,000	$64,304	36	$2,000	$603,874
16	$2,000	$72,735	37	$2,000	$666,262
17	$2,000	$82,008	38	$2,000	$734,888
18	$2,000	$92,209	39	$2,000	$810,376
19	$2,000	$103,430	40	$2,000	$893,414
20	$2,000	$115,773	41	$2,000	$984,755
21	$2,000	$129,350	42	$2,000	$1,085,231

"That can't be right," Joe protested. He drew a laptop computer from his attache case and deftly punched in the necessary formulas and figures to set up a spreadsheet.

"$1,085,231," he declared. "Well, I'll be. I've never really looked at it that way."

"Most smokers don't either, Joe. It costs a lot of money to experience the health consequences of smoking, though."

Joe was about to say something, but stopped. Robert continued to make his point.

"Consider the example of a 23-year-old pack-a-day Canadian smoker who quits and invests the savings at a tax-sheltered rate of 10%, say in a Canadian Registered Retirement Savings Plan. She'll have $1,000,000 by retirement at age 65. For an American smoker the equivalent figure is $250,000 U.S. dollars, based on saving $800 annually. And let's not forget that tobacco taxes will probably increase in years to come."

"It's not easy to get a 10% return on your money, tax-free," Joe objected.

"But paying off personal debt or mortgages can save a person the same amount of money, if a tax-sheltered investment isn't available," Robert said.

"People don't think like that," Joe said. "They'd just blow the money on something else, instead of investing it."

"I hear that from smokers all the time, Joe. I tell them to spend a week in Hawaii every year by all means, or trade in their old car every so often. There are also many organizations that can turn the cost of one pack of cigarettes per day into food, education and health care for needy children."

Joe was every bit as insistent as Robert.

"Robert, you don't get it," he said. "Smokers want their pleasure *right now*. They don't see the costs you mention, they don't see the future, and I've no idea how much they care about hungry kids on the other side of the planet."

"You may be right," said Robert. "Some people don't have a head for figures. But there's an easy way for them to appreciate the dollar-cost of their habit. All they have to do is collect all their cigarette butts in a large glass jar for two or three weeks. They must put an amount of money equal to what they spend on smoking into another jar, daily.

"As time passes they can simply compare the jar of butts with the jar of bucks. I'm told the jar of butts with a bit of water added makes a dandy aid to quitting. A sniff of the contents apparently smells worse than it sounds, and helps to deal with cravings to smoke."

"No doubt," Joe half-heartedly agreed. They seemed to be getting nowhere.

"Maybe it's a good thing that so many people smoke," Robert said, changing his strategy. "According to a study commissioned by one major tobacco company, smokers cost the medical system less than non-smokers. I happen to have a news item about it somewhere." He shuffled through some papers on his desk.

"Yes, here it is. 'Anti-smoking groups rarely consider the reduction in health costs resulting from the premature death of certain smokers. A person who dies from lung cancer at age 70 will not be hospitalized later with another disease.' What do you think, Joe? Perhaps state health insurance plans should distribute free cigarettes!"

Joe was not amused. "So why are we being sued for the costs of treating diseases caused by smoking?" he asked.

"Beats me." Robert said. "Do you think there's been some kind of misunderstanding?"

Joe gave a non-committal snort.

"All right, Joe. Sleep on it. You have to admit one thing, though. Smokers might want to keep the conclusion of that study at their yellowed fingertips. They can use it to reassure concerned non-smokers who fret about tobacco draining the health-care bucket."

Joe stared hard at Robert, then finally chuckled and shook his head in mock disbelief.

"You're in the wrong business, Robert. You should have been in advertising."

Robert laughed. "Thanks!" he said. "I'm only trying to sell you on not smoking, after all. Perhaps we can close the deal soon. But let's not talk about money anymore. How was your Valentine's weekend with Robin?"

"It was wonderful. A bit rushed, though. There never seems to be enough time."

"I suppose that means you didn't complete your last assignment, then?" Robert asked.

"Actually, no," Joe said. "But I've given it some thought."

"And have you thought about why you still smoke?" Robert asked.

Joe didn't say anything. He got up, took the few steps to the window, and looked out on the dying day. "I don't know all my reasons for doing things," he finally said. "I just seem to roll on day after day." He turned around to face back into the room, leaning with his elbows on the window-sill. His hands were stuck out in front of him, palms upward, as though he were weighing alternatives.

"There's no way I could stop and keep my position. Can you imagine the news items? *Well-Known Tobacco Figurehead Quits Smoking.* No, I don't think so."

"I rather doubt they'd say that," Robert suggested. "What about something a bit more dramatic like *'Hamel Kicks the Kamel,'* or *'May-I-Borrow Man Settles His Debt?'*"

"Settles his debt?" Joe asked with raised eyebrows. "That would mean more than quitting smoking. You know, sometimes I wish I'd never started smoking, and never worked for Tobacco. What would I do for a living, though?"

"Good question. Just what would you do for a living?" Robert blurted out. It was a bit unfair to imply that Joe had no morals where money was concerned, but it had an effect.

Joe blinked.

"I get your point," he said, back on his feet now. "I get it. Right in a sore spot, in fact. I've had to sink pretty low to get high up in this business, but I'm getting ready for a change."

He retrieved his jacket and made ready to leave.

"I can't stay longer today, Robert. Don't worry, I know you're trying to help. I'll be back."

"Okay, Joe, that's no problem. You're doing fine. I know you'll do the best you can, whatever happens."

"You bet I will," said Joe. "See you next week."

With that he left.

* * * * *

Robert made an entry in the clinical record:

Joe was in a fighting mood today, fresh from a stockholder's meeting. So after reviewing the financial cost of smoking we had a little scrap but parted friends.

The surgery and the government hearings are coming up, major events. I get the feeling that Joe is going to do something soon, but I'm not exactly sure what. There's more on his mind than quitting smoking.

Next week: we'll see.

9

Signals To Smoke

You need only to claim the events of your life to make yourself yours. When you truly possess all you have been and done, which may take some time, you are fierce with reality.
— Florida Scott-Maxwell

February 24th

JOE ARRIVED RIGHT ON TIME for the next session, whistling the tune of The Tobacco-Brain Blues as he hung up his coat. He took his seat, toying with his well-worn lighter as he and Robert chatted briefly about the weather, the news, and other daily distractions.

Then Joe casually announced, "Today I want you to tell me exactly how to get ready to quit."

The promise of sharp steel had prodded Joe into action. His cancer was ready to be cut out, and his doctors had strongly advised him to stop for at least a week before the surgery. He was willing to make a stab at quitting.

"Congratulations!" Robert said. "I had a feeling you might be ready to take that step."

"Everywhere I turn," Joe said. "people are telling me to stop smoking. I might as well try before this operation. You know, doc, they say I might even be completely cured if this gamble pays off."

"That's fantastic, Joe. Shall we get started then? We've got some work to do."

Robert dug out a single sheet from the carpet of paper on his desk.

"Here, Joe. These are the essentials of stopping smoking. This is a plan that has worked for many others."

"That's great," Joe said after reading it. "I've been keeping track of each cigarette, like you suggested. Here, have a look at the results."

Joe opened his briefcase and produced about a dozen dog-eared index cards. Robert spread them out on the table and scanned the entries. He took a fresh piece of paper and wrote 'Triggers' across the top.

- List the pros and cons of smoking, as well as those of not smoking.
- Identify the situations and circumstances (triggers) that lead to smoking. Plan to avoid or change them for several months after quitting.
- Get support for quitting from everybody possible.
- Exercise. Physical activity calms the mind and body, and helps you to lose weight.
- Remember that quitting is very possible, and is very powerful medicine for the body and soul.
- Use nicotine replacement, if appropriate.
- Stop smoking.
- Reward and congratulate yourself.
- Replace the pleasure of smoking with other more enjoyable and satisfying activities.
- Note the benefits of not smoking.
- Remember that quitting is a process and takes time. Relapses are learning opportunities.
- Don't stop stopping until you've stopped forever.

"Look at this, Joe. You frequently smoke while driving." He noted that down. "And while talking on the phone. And after meals." The inventory of triggers grew longer. "With coffee. During meetings at work. When feeling anxious. To concentrate. First thing in the morning. When talking on the phone." Eventually the ten most common circumstances of Joe's smoking were listed. "These are your triggers, your commands to smoke."

"I don't quite buy that," Joe said. "I certainly don't smoke *every* time I drive somewhere."

"No, but this is a really important point. One of the keys to survival is to realize how 'triggers' to smoking are created, and how to avoid or change them." Robert put down his pen. "Let's look at that. First, do you remember how non-smokers become regular smokers?"

"Sure. They try tobacco out of curiosity, then begin to experiment by smoking in different situations and moods. They might discover some of the small benefits of smoking, like increased concentration on monotonous tasks, or perhaps decreased appetite. Maybe it reduces their anxiety or provides some stimulation."

"Well said, Joe. But then unwary smokers find themselves addicted, smoking regularly. They're trained to smoke. When you think about it, a smoker learns his or her habit in much the same way that a dog learns to sit on command."

Joe looked a bit doubtful.

"The dog hears the command, sits down, and gets a dog biscuit. The pattern is *command, behavior, and then a reward*. According to your records you often smoke in your car. You drive away, light up, and receive nicotine. Over time, driving has become a trigger to your smoking."

"I see," said Joe. "Triggers are like commands that contribute to the urge to smoke. If smokers obey and light up, they quickly get their reward, nicotine."

"Exactly, Joe. And don't forget that nicotine reaches the brain almost instantly after it's inhaled. The reward is fast and consistent, which is why smoking is so addictive.

"After a few years of smoking, nicotine will have been paired up millions of times with the act of inhaling from a cigarette. That's powerful training. *Your brain comes to expect nicotine whenever you encounter your triggers.*"

Joe produced his cigarette pack and set it on the table.

"You're suggesting I'm like some kind of trained animal, like a Pavlov dog drooling every time the bell rings," he said. "I don't agree with that. Have you got any evidence to back up your claim?"

"No disrespect intended, Joe, but it's been shown that smokers' hearts may beat faster at the mere sight of a cigarette package," said Robert.

Joe laughed. "That reminds me of how hungry I get around the smell of food," he said, "or how fast my dog comes running when I rattle the dog biscuit box."

"Exactly. Basically, a smoker's body comes to expect nicotine whenever a trigger is encountered. The brain thinks *Aha! Nicotine is served!*"

Joe nodded. "Okay. I get it."

"Even moods can become 'triggers,' Robert explained. Many nicotine-addicted people learn that the irritability and anxiety of nicotine withdrawal can be relieved by smoking. In other words, withdrawal symptoms become signals for them to smoke."

"I know," Joe said. "I know all about nicotine. What about my situation? What should I try to avoid?"

"Have a look at this table of other common smoking triggers, besides nicotine withdrawal symptoms." Robert retrieved an article from his files and flipped it open to show a table:

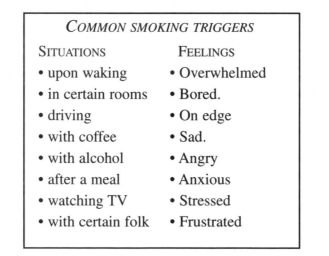

COMMON SMOKING TRIGGERS	
SITUATIONS	FEELINGS
• upon waking	• Overwhelmed
• in certain rooms	• Bored.
• driving	• On edge
• with coffee	• Sad.
• with alcohol	• Angry
• after a meal	• Anxious
• watching TV	• Stressed
• with certain folk	• Frustrated

Joe looked it over. "I see your point now. Triggers can be pretty subtle," he observed.

"Yes, they can. But they always get their power from being associated with nicotine. It's an addictive drug."

The issue of smoking and quitting somehow kept coming back to nicotine. It was the reward that people smoked for. The urge to smoke resulted from withdrawal symptoms, or situations so commonly associated with nicotine that they had almost become commands to smoke.

"I suppose that combining two or more triggers can create a pretty strong craving," Joe said.

"Sure. Imagine how tempting it might be to smoke with alcohol, with coffee, after a meal, and while feeling bored. That would be like ordering our well-trained dog to *sit, stay, and be quiet.* He won't move. In the same way, a smoker experiences a strong urge to light up when faced with more than one trigger."

Joe was nodding in agreement with each point made.

"Joe, you might want to avoid your triggers for a while after quitting, or inactivate them somehow. If driving is a trigger, consider changing that by cleaning the interior of your car and removing the ashtrays. If coffee breaks are triggers, what about a travel mug and going for a short coffee walk rather than sitting down as usual? There's many ways to deal with these situations, once you've identified them."

"That makes sense. What about triggers to *not* smoke?"

"Well, a trigger to *not* smoke would be a situation where *not* smoking is consistently rewarded," said Robert, "or in which you don't usually smoke.

"I've got my list of those," Joe said. "When busy with my hands. When playing sports. When I'm very happy. When I'm spending time with my kids. Walking in the rain. Riding my bicycle, or motorcycle. There are more, too."

"Great. Use that information to avoid cravings. Spend as much time as possible in those situations. It's also a good idea to get people around you to provide support and encouragement for not smoking. And keep the negative consequences of smoking in mind."

Joe commented that he had never realized the essentials of quitting were so simple.

"Well, quitting *is* simple, Joe," Robert assured him. "A smoker doesn't need to spend their life savings on two weeks in a no-smoke spa eating freshly-squeezed wheat grass while standing on their head getting hypnotically acupunctured. Simply follow the approach I've outlined, and *do it*."

"Just like that…. I've never felt so ready to quit," said Joe. "At the same time, it's a bit scary."

"That's understandable, Joe. Cigarettes have been there for you all your life, through thick and thin. You count on them. Quitting is almost like abandoning a loyal friend and there's often some grieving the loss. The power of triggers also outlasts the physical nicotine withdrawal, which fades out over two or three weeks. Quitting can seem quite frightening, until you make friends with your smoke-free self."

Joe sighed wearily. "I understand the whole mess, but I'm not completely sure I can get out of it."

"That's okay," Robert said. "Just do your best. Quitting smoking has life-or-death consequences. Freedom is the goal, Joe. Besides surviving, ex-smokers often experience a new sense of confidence and power. Quitting may be difficult, but it's possible. It's good medicine for the soul.

"Don't allow yourself to think about failure. Millions of heavy smokers have already quit. Conquering nicotine addiction is a matter of strategy and perseverance. If the first few attempts aren't successful, pay attention to what caused the so-called failure, change it, and then try, try again."

"Okay. You're right. I can do it. I'll quit, or die trying."

"Fantastic. Is five days from now a good time to stop?"

"Saturday?" Joe thought for a moment. "Yeah, I should be able to keep myself busy, and stay away from triggers."

"And one last thing, Joe. Let's make this your next assignment. Make lists of your reasons to smoke, and not smoke." Robert drew a balance on a sheet of paper and made a few entries. "Arrange your reasons like this, and add to them whenever new ones occur to you. It helps to keep the big picture in mind."

"Hey, I like that," said Joe. "I can see right away that 'I like to smoke' would go in the lower left-hand box as one of the 'pros of smoking.' I suppose the health risks are part of the 'cons of smoking.' This looks like it could be a very interesting assignment."

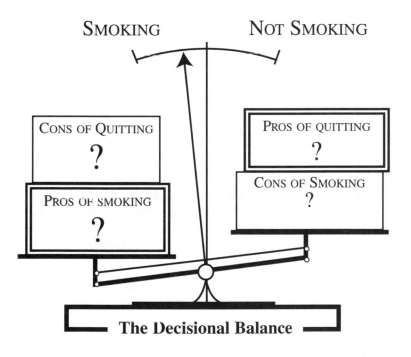

The Decisional Balance

"Speaking of assignments, how's that other one going?"

"The one on women and smoking? Very well. Very interesting. I've been getting some help, of course. From Robin," Joe added in answer to Robert's questioning look. "She's meeting me here tonight, actually."

"Wonderful! I look forward to seeing her again."

Robert then reviewed some practical details. "Cut down a little before quitting, but not too much. Keep paying attention to when and where you smoke, and plan to avoid those situations. Save all your butts and put them in a large glass jar. Don't deny yourself the smoke-breaks you used to take, but just don't smoke during them. Get a five-minute egg-timer. Whenever you get the urge to smoke, start it running. The urges will pass, if you just wait. Set the timer and simply relax for five minutes."

Robert handed Joe some instructions for nicotine replacement. "And use this. It works."

Robin had been sitting in the waiting room, and she rose to greet Robert when he showed Joe to the door.

"Dr. Borenot? You're looking very well," she said. "Congratulations on your change of career. And thank you so much for helping Joe. I swear he's worth it."

The trio exchanged some small talk, and then Robert returned to his office to write the clinical note for the day. As he sat down at his desk he knocked his pen to the floor, and stooped to retrieve it. It was then he couldn't help noticing a paper under Joe's chair. Robert's eyes grew wider as he read the copied memos, clearly marked "CONFIDENTIAL":

"In a sense, the tobacco industry may be thought of as being a highly specialized, highly ritualized and stylized segment of the pharmaceutical industry. Tobacco products, uniquely, contain and deliver nicotine, a potent drug with a variety of physiological effects."

"Evidence is now available to indicate that the 14- to 18-year-old group is an increasing segment of the smoking population. RJR-T must soon establish a successful new brand in this market if our position in the industry is to be maintained over the long term.

January β∂, ˙çβ74"

The exact date was hard to make out, but the year seemed to be 1974. That would have been sometime before the introduction of the "Joe Camel" promotion in 1988, Robert realized. (Before that marketing, 1 in 200 teen smokers used Camel cigarettes. Two years into the campaign, it was 1 in 3. Ninety-one percent of six-year-olds came to recognize Joe Camel, and associate him with cigarettes.)

Robert re-read the two passages until he had memorized the words. The notes seemed harmless, unless you considered that the tobacco industry unanimously maintained that nicotine was not addictive, and that their advertising was not aimed at children. The memos contradicted that stand, which had been repeated under oath by industry executives.

Perhaps Joe had left the paper there intentionally. If not, what was he doing with it in his briefcase? And what now?

The clock striking nine startled Robert. He'd been sitting there for over an hour since Joe and Robin left. He put the incriminating document in Joe's chart and slipped it in his briefcase, intending to write the daily entry at home after a late supper. He was tired though, and eventually went to bed without completing the clinical record.

Robert slept badly that night. He dreamt of a pack of bloodhounds chasing their quarry through the night. Their eyes glowed red and their breath streamed like smoke behind them in the cool night air. In the early hours of the morning, he was awakened by his dog growling at something outside. Robert looked, but saw nothing there.

* * * * *

The next morning Robert finally made the chart entry:

Joe has decided to stop smoking. He's booked for surgery in two weeks, and that seems to have tipped the scales. He's definitely moved into the 'action' stage now, with a target date for quitting in just five days.

He understands his habit well, which should help him to quit. On the other hand, he's under a great deal of stress. Besides the surgery, he must be concerned about his scheduled appearance at the upcoming government hearings.

Like every smoker, he has reasons to smoke and reasons not to. Like every smoker, he deserves not to.

In this preparation stage, my job is to support him and provide specific instructions and techniques.

Next week: Follow-up to quitting. Stress management?

10

Stress Mismanagement

Although the world is full of suffering,
it is also full of the overcoming of it.
— Helen Keller

THE NEXT DAY Robert arrived at his office to find it ransacked. Nothing seemed to have been destroyed or damaged, but drawers and files were spilled out and scattered as though somebody had been searching through them. The police detectives examined the room and dusted for fingerprints. "It wasn't the cleaning lady," one suggested. "The alarms were disarmed, the locks were cleanly picked, and there are no prints."

Robert called a locksmith to re-key the locks, and his lawyer to notify all his clients that their records had been illegally accessed. He spent the better part of the next three days cleaning up the mess. Nothing seemed to be missing, but anything could have been photographed.

* * * * *

March 3rd

WHEN HE ARRIVED for the next session Joe looked very concerned. He paced about the room peering distractedly at the paintings and decorations before settling down.

"Congratulations on Day 3 smoke-free, Joe," Robert said warmly. "How goes the battle?" This was a critical time for his client. Many people who quit smoking start again within the first ten days, when the symptoms of nicotine withdrawal are at their worst.

"It's not as bad as I thought," said Joe, "but I'm jumpier than a cricket on uppers."

"That's to be expected, Joe, to a certain extent. Are you sleeping okay?"

"I've been having some strange dreams. Surgery and blood, that sort of thing. But I feel pretty good about myself."

"Hey, you should. Congratulations again, Joe. Tell me

more about how it's going."

Joe explained how he was avoiding his triggers. The car had been thoroughly cleaned and flowers now sprung out of the empty ashtrays. After meals, he'd go for a short walk. He found it helped to stay busy, and active.

The most troublesome part of Joe's nicotine withdrawal was a general feeling of anxiety. He'd already resorted to sniffing his foul-smelling jar of cigarette butts once, when the urge to smoke became dangerously strong as he was reviewing some documents.

"That's those empty nicotine receptors acting up," Robert said. "The nicotine patch isn't meant to totally replace the amount one gets from smoking."

Joe looked away. He was holding his lighter, rolling it over and over and occasionally flicking the top open and shut. He seemed unusually agitated, even for somebody in nicotine withdrawal. Maybe something else was bothering him. Those documents?

"What do you think would be most helpful for us to do today?" Robert asked.

"Tell me how to manage stress."

"Quit smoking," Robert said.

"I did that," said Joe, slightly irritated. "And that's no way to handle stress."

"Well, yes and no. It seems that on average, smokers report lower stress levels several months after quitting. On the other hand, they say that smoking calms them down. What do you make of that?"

"Say again?"

"When they are smoking regularly, people find that a cigarette can help them to feel a bit more relaxed. Let's suppose it reduces their stress level from 7 to 5 HU's — that's hassle units — on a scale of 10. Now, suppose these smokers report an average stress level of about 6 HU's. Months after having quit, they report an average stress level of 4. So what do you make of that?"

Joe pondered the question.

"Could smoking have been causing them some stress? Perhaps going into nicotine withdrawal several times a day is stressful? Wait a minute, that's definitely stressful. That would explain those results. Is that it?"

"Probably, Joe."

"Well, I'll be. Smoking causes stress. What a rip-off! But it also helps in the short term."

"The very short term, Joe. Then about half an hour after smoking, when the level of nicotine in the blood has fallen by about half, it's withdrawal time again."

"And that's a trigger!" Joe exclaimed.

"Exactly. You've got the bull by the horns now, Joe."

"Good. Now tell me, good doctor, what next? How can a fellow effectively handle tension and harassment?"

"I'm glad you asked. That's an important topic. Are you familiar with the body's response to stress?"

"Sort of."

"Then you know that during times of stress your body pumps adrenaline and other hormones into the bloodstream. Your heart speeds up and your blood pressure increases, in preparation for fighting or fleeing.

"That state of 'red alert' is harmful if it goes on for too long. Every body needs time out occasionally. Think of an army, Joe. The soldiers lose their edge if they're always on full alert. Relaxation between periods of intense activity is as essential as sleep."

"But people don't always choose to be stressed, Robert. I certainly don't," Joe said.

"Things might happen that are outside your control, like the weather. On the other hand, you can choose to wear a raincoat or use an umbrella when it rains. Stress management is similar. There's not much point blaming the rain when the problem is you're not wearing a raincoat."

Robert thought for a bit before responding.

"So where do I get a new raincoat? How can I deal with high levels of stress?"

"Sometimes medication helps. But that can be like blowing away the smoke without putting out the fire. Medication sometimes just treats the symptoms, not the source. One of the best ways to handle stress is to make time to recover between crises." Robert dug into his freshly-organized files and pulled out a graph.

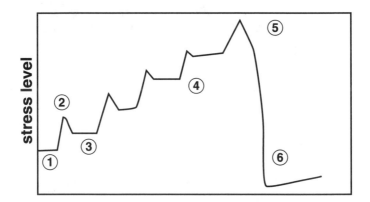

Figure 1. Pattern of escalating stress.
Point 1: Normal stress level. No sweat.
Point 2: Minor emergency increases stress. Yikes!
Point 3: Stress level stays high; inadequate relaxation.
Point 4: Anxiety builds up. Things are getting tense.
Point 5: Total nervous breakdown. Hospitalization.
Point 6: Slow recovery.

"This shows how a person's stress level changes over time. Look at the pattern here. The higher the stress-level, the higher the line goes. Notice that it goes up and down but never gets back down to the original level."

Robert pointed out the features with a pen as he mentioned them.

"This is not good stress management. When somebody already feels pressured, they don't handle further problems very well. There isn't enough recovery after each crisis. The anxiety level goes up each time, but then doesn't come all the way back down again. The anxiety can eventually build up into a full-blown breakdown."

"I sort of get it. It's a bit hard to imagine."

"Good idea. Why don't you try *imagining* it, Joe. Let's use some hypnosis again, if that's all right with you."

Joe agreed, and made himself comfortable.

"Close your eyes, feel your breath flowing in and out as though it had a life of its own...." Robert spoke softly in a measured cadence. "You feel yourself going deeper and deeper into a relaxing trance, with every breath...." His client was soon fully hypnotized.

"Imagine you're a busy single parent by the name of Jack Kantrelax, preparing to feed and bathe your infant child. Suddenly you're distracted by the telephone ringing. You answer." Robert passed the cell phone to Joe and speed-dialed it from his desk-set.

"Hello?" Joe said, answering.

"Mr. Kantrelax?"

"Yes."

"Mr. Kantrelax, It's my privilege to tell you about our special introductory once-in-a-lifetime offer. Would you be interested in more information?"

"About what?"

Robert left the phone off the hook and continued his guided tour of poor stress management.

"Before you can hear what the amazing offer is about, the baby's milk warming on the kitchen stove boils over and the steam triggers the central smoke alarm." Robert sounded the alarm on his desk clock, and placed it on the headrest of Joe's chair. "This sets off the even louder baby. Waaaaaaaahhhh! Waaaaaaahhhhhh!" he added in a high falsetto tone that set his own teeth on edge.

To judge from Joe's horrified expression, he had little enthusiasm for returning to child-rearing and was experiencing significant stress at this point.

"You attempt to calm the terrified child. Suddenly 50 gallons of water flood the living room as the ceiling collapses. You forgot the bathtub filling upstairs!

"You dash upstairs to find the bathroom door swollen shut. By this point you really aren't thinking straight. You grab the household shotgun to blow open the stuck door. Overkill perhaps, but two barrels of buckshot quickly solves the problem." Robert took two large books and slammed them on the table. *Blam! Blam!"*

Joe grabbed his chair.

"Suddenly a band of armed thieves smash through your front door. You defend your child and home, firing wildly in their general direction."

Joe quickly stood up, knocking the alarm clock to the floor where it promptly died. His breathing was becoming short and shallow.

"It's all right, Joe. Easy. It's okay now. Sit down."

The poor man sat down but was twitching alarmingly. Robert had a horrible vision of a headline:

"TOBACCO EXECUTIVE IN NICOTINE WITHDRAWAL
DIES DURING CLINICAL HYPNOSIS."

"Relax, Joe. It's not as bad as you thought. The fire fighters arrived and heard the baby. They saw smoke spewing from the kitchen exhaust fan, so they bashed through the locked front door with their axes and swarmed inside. Twenty pounds of fire retardant foam easily extinguished the scorched saucepan of milk.

"Your marksmanship was mercifully inaccurate. Although the hoses on one fire truck would never hold water again, the fire chief escaped with only minor injuries."

Joe seemed to be tolerating the stress a bit better now.

"To make a long story short, the SWAT team and your lawyer finally leave, and the baby gets fed. Instead of taking a well-deserved break though, you chain-smoke while immediately patching up the entrance to your home using the water-damaged rosewood table from the dining room.

"That night you lie in bed worrying obsessively about the events of the day and working your way through an entire pack of Slayer's King Size Fill-Tar-Tip cigarettes. After finally falling asleep you dream that your smoking has started the house on fire. Sure enough, you wake to the screech of the smoke alarm and a posse of vengeful firefighters gleefully pounding down the remains of your front door.

"The very next day you arrange for the necessary home repairs with the first available contractor. To cover those costs and the damage to the fire truck, you accept a night job at the zoo extracting poisonous venom from pit vipers. That's in addition to your regular day job as an air traffic controller at a busy airport, incidentally.

"Stress starts to take its toll, and you find it difficult to concentrate. Work piles up at the zoo and so you bring some home in your briefcase. In a classic example of mistaken efficiency, you catch a few winks at the wheel. Fortunately nobody's seriously injured in the accident that ensues, and the snakes are eventually recaptured."

It was time to wind down the lesson.

"It seems that you might be able to cope after all, but then on the same day you receive notice of your adjusted house and car insurance premiums, and the bills for the renovations and the fire truck repairs. After calculating that by working twenty four hours a day you might have them paid off by the middle of the next century, you finally lose control and suffer a major breakdown."

At this point Robert figured that Joe, who was grasping onto his chair as though it was his only connection to the known universe, had a firm understanding of unrelieved stress. It was now time to bring him back to his relatively relaxed reality.

"At the count of three you'll wake up slowly, Joe. You'll remember all the feelings and events of the hypnosis. One, two, three."

Joe visibly relaxed a notch or two as he regained his usual state of consciousness.

"My God," he said, wild-eyed. "I feel like I've aged fifty years, and badly, at that. Not a pleasant experience!"

"'Sorry about that, Joe. But do you see my point about unrelieved stress?"

"As clear as the nose on my face, Robert. That was one constant crisis."

"Thankfully there's a healthier way to handle stressful situations, Joe. Catch your breath and have a look at this next graph, in comparison to the first." Robert handed him another page. "You can see that the stress level will not build up over the long run, if a person takes time out to recover between crises."

"That's great in theory," said Joe after absorbing the concept, "although when you're up to your butt in alligators, as they say, it's a bit late to think of draining the swamp!"

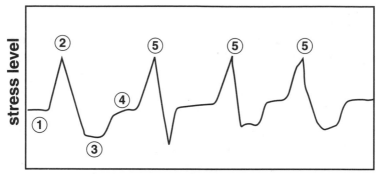

Figure 2. Effective stress management
Point 1: Everything's fine. Smooth sailing.
Point 2: Suddenly the stress level increases. Bad hair day.
Point 3: Crisis passes. Time-out for recovery. Chill out.
Point 4: Stress level returns to normal. Ready for anything.
Point 5: Further crises are well handled, with full recovery.

"But if you're stuck in the swamp, Joe, the sooner you learn how to wrestle alligators the better. There are many ways to handle stress besides smoking. There's self-hypnosis, music, re-framing of problems, physical relaxation, exercise, humor, sharing of feelings and problems, and so on."

"Who's got time for that? You're suggesting a facial for people ready to jump out of their skins."

"And that might be just what they need, Joe. Small adjustments in lifestyle can really reduce stress levels."

Joe flicked his lighter open and shut, alternately striking sparks and snuffing the flame. "And you're sure that smoking doesn't help?" he asked.

"Joe, believe me, the misery and stress caused by smoking is as bad as any I've ever seen, and I've been around."

Joe's eyes narrowed as though he was remembering

something distressing, then his face softened. "Tell me more," he said.

"Well, if you always rely on smoking to handle stress, you forget many other techniques and don't develop new ones. Like unused muscles, your other coping skills waste away if they don't get exercised."

Joe nodded, thoughtfully. Robert then offered to demonstrate, again through hypnosis, how Jack Kantrelax could have managed his situation more effectively.

"Uh, no thanks, Doc. Just tell me about it."

"Okay. The phone rings. The milk boils over. The fire alarm goes off. Jack hangs up the phone and opens the window to clear the air. He takes a deep breath of fresh air, and gets some oxygen to his brain so he can think straight."

"The baby wails and the ceiling collapses, but Jack silences the fire alarm and calls off the firemen. Perhaps he would even have remembered or heard the bathtub filling and turned the taps off in time.

"With the household once again under control Jack settles down to a well-deserved breather, 'time out' in his hectic day. He enjoys some mellow music and a soothing cup of tea instead of a smoke.

"Over the next month he always manages to find some way of unwinding between periods of high activity and anxiety. You might say that occasionally spending some time on the bench allows him to play the game of life with gusto, but without burning out. He's more effective at solving and preventing problems.

"Do you see how that might work?" asked Robert.

"Yeah, that's much better." Joe said. He thought for a few moments, and his forehead regained its wrinkled, concerned look. "But this is almost the twenty-first century," he said. "Time is money. Nobody can stay that cool."

"It's true that we live in hurried times," Robert admitted. "which means there's all the more benefit to be had from quiet reflection, sharing with friends, exercise, sports, meditation, listening to music, short walks, or contemplation of art and beauty. Life can be much less stressful if one develops a healthy diet, a strong sense of purpose and goals, a rich spiritual life, and solid connections with family and friends. The object is presumably to enjoy life, not rush through it to an early conclusion."

Robert wasn't sure he was getting anywhere. Joe was definitely distracted today. "Anyway, that's just one way to look at it," Robert suggested. "What do you think?"

Joe considered the matter for a few moments. "What you say makes sense," he replied, "but it's not that simple. There's something more."

"Something more?"

"That sense of purpose you mentioned. That's the main thing. People cope with all kinds of stress when they believe in what they're doing."

"How true. Do you believe in what you do, Joe?"

"Most of it," he replied, then looked away to stare out the window.

"Is there something on your mind, Joe?" Robert prompted eventually. "The surgery next week?"

Joe hesitated before replying.

"No. I'll take that as it comes. I was just thinking that you may be right about stress management, but you've got the wrong approach to smokers."

"How so?"

"I don't think that smokers today really care about the harmful effects of smoking. Not enough to stop smoking, anyway. They don't want to live forever. They just want to feel good while they're alive."

Robert listened, and nodded. Joe continued.

"You talk a lot about the benefits of quitting, and the damage smoking does. But I don't think kids care about dying in forty years, or thirty, or even twenty. They haven't lived long enough to have experienced any future consequences on that time scale. And people of any age struggling to cope don't care what happens twenty years from now. If they think that smoking helps them today, they'll do it."

Robert listened intently as Joe explained his perspective.

"People want good lives, not long ones. We offer them a great life. Shorter perhaps, but what glory, man! The guy in the tobacco advertisement steps out of his race car and grabs the trophy. He's strong, independent, and takes calculated risks. That's just what appeals to kids, apparently. We don't sponsor knitting bees, Robert. Go figure. We sell an addictive, harmful product, but an independent, healthy image."

Robert wasn't sure what to make of Joe being so forthcoming. It was quite a dramatic change.

"I don't think the anti-tobacco folks really understand," Joe continued. "Tobacco is a worldwide business. We're among the largest corporations in the United States, and we spend billions of dollars annually on promotion. We could probably sell sand in the desert, if we added nicotine to it and had free rein to advertise."

"You're not proud of that," Robert suggested.

Joe looked a bit puzzled. They'd stumbled into unfamiliar territory, some new possibility opened up by Joe having stopped smoking. Just then the phone rang. Apparently a courier needed Robert's signature for a delivery. "Will you excuse me a moment, Joe?" he asked, and stepped out briefly to take care of the matter.

His client was just straightening up beside his chair when Robert returned. "Dropped my lighter," Joe explained, resuming his seat.

Robert picked up the thread of their conversation, tugging it a bit to see what might unravel. "You were just saying you could sell sand in the desert, Joe. You're an expert in marketing, and I was just thinking. How would you go about reducing the number of smokers, if you wanted to?"

Joe was silent, seeming to consider the question or perhaps something else. He looked straight at Robert for a moment before answering.

"That'd be pretty simple, Robert. First off, you'd have to spend a few billion dollars every year on your campaign, like we do now promoting tobacco. It wouldn't take much to get the facts out in public, say ten thousand explicit billboards, full page ads in the major papers, and a few well-placed television spots.

"On the other hand I'm not sure just the facts would do the trick. People are basically dreamers, you know? They believe what they want. You'd do well to get some rock stars and sports figures on board. Buy some glamour in Hollywood for the concept of not smoking. Offer free exercise classes and nutritional counseling to anybody concerned about their weight and appearance." He paused.

"And buy back the politicians. Get them out of tobacco promotion, and into raising taxes on tobacco products. Tobacco works for most people because it's cheap. I don't think it would at ten bucks a pack, especially for kids. They are quite price-sensitive, as we say in the industry. That's it, Robert. You'd probably cut the number of smokers by half in about five years."

What an extraordinary outburst for Joe, still a tobacco industry figurehead! He seemed relieved, leaning back to watch Robert's reaction.

"That's a great pipe dream," said Robert, testing. "Things might change a little over the next while, but not that much."

"Hey, Robert. I stopped smoking. Things do change.

Keep the faith." *Beautiful,* Robert thought.

"That's absolutely right. Congratulations again, Joe!" he said. "You've made wonderful progress."

Their time was up for the day. Robert asked about the assignments, only to learn that Joe had been too busy to work on them. They discussed Joe's impending surgery.

"I hope all goes smoothly for you next week," Robert said, warmly clasping Joe's hand in parting.

"Thanks." Joe placed his hand on Robert's shoulder. "Thanks for everything."

* * * * *

As usual, Robert wrote a note in Joe's chart:

Joe seemed less unstable than last week. He hasn't smoked at all. He's doing great.

We had an extraordinary session today reviewing stress management, in which he volunteered how he would go about reducing tobacco usage.

I am delighted with his progress.

Next week: No session. Joe's surgery.

11

Stepping Towards Light

What saves a man is to take a step. Then another step. It is always the same step, but you have to take it.

— Saint-Exupéry

March 10th

SOMETHING UNFORESEEN HAPPENED in the final stages of Joe's surgery.

He'd quit smoking on his target date, exactly as planned, and by the time he checked into the hospital could already breathe a bit easier. The anesthetist Dr. Ann Swift explained how he would be "put to sleep," and the surgeons reviewed their plans with him one last time. There was a good possibility he would be cured.

The operation went smoothly until it was almost over. Joe suddenly found himself regaining consciousness and lifting away from the table, rising and turning slowly over until, in slow motion, he could see the doctors reacting below him.

Ann said something urgent to the surgeons that made them immediately stop and look up from their work. An alarm sounded from the anesthetic machine. She searched for a pulse in Joe's neck, found none, and swore softly. The heart monitor now showed a flat line where there should have been a regular heartbeat. Reaching over the sterile operating field, she thumped Joe's chest with a clenched and determined fist.

Nothing happened.

The paddles were already in place on Joe's chest. Ann called out "Clear!" as she charged the defibrillator. Electricity streamed through Joe's heart, but it stayed stubbornly stopped.

The defibrillation was repeated. Again nothing. Ann emptied a loaded syringe into the intravenous line as one of the surgeons began rhythmically pumping his chest. "Shall we open him?" asked another, prepared to cut down between Joe's ribs to expose his heart. Then he would massage it with his hand, doing for Joe what his own heart could not.

"No, we'll try pacing him first," Ann said.

As though the ceiling were holding him down in this world, Joe stopped rising. A bright light swelled and flared around him. He heard voices calling, turned to look, and saw the figures. He heard a question. It shocked him. His heart suddenly wanted to burst.

"Hold it!" Ann directed. All eyes in the room looked to the heart monitor, and all movement stopped. There was a heartbeat now. There was a pulse.

Joe felt himself slowly sinking back to the table, feet first, until his toe landed precisely where it appeared to stick out from the disrupted surgical drapes. Ann exclaimed, "Okay! Okay! He's back!"

There was an excited buzz as the surgeons swiftly finished their work and Ann stabilized Joe's hold on life. Minutes later he was whisked to the intensive care unit.

Robin had been waiting nervously during the operation and was stunned to hear the news. She was somewhat reassured by seeing Joe in the ICU, stable and responsive. He couldn't talk much, with the drugs still sedating him, but he was alive and breathing on his own. He'd be fine, the doctors assured her.

There didn't appear to have been any damage done to his heart, but nobody could explain why it had stopped like that.

Outside in the early spring weather, patients tethered to their intravenous machines were clustered about the hospital's main entrance, smoking. After visiting Joe, Robin sat in the coffee shop overlooking the scene, and was seized by a bizarre craving to have a cigarette *right now*.

She thought back over the course of her smoking history. Tobacco had practically been a member of her family. *I'm just going to pick up the kids from school. Don't forget to buy cigarettes! Mummy can't play with you right now, Robin. She's having her smoke.*

Smoking had seemed as natural to her as breathing, something you just do without thinking too much about it. There was no ignoring the effects as they began to catch up with her though. In her early twenties she noticed a worsening in her morning coughs, and an increasing shortness of breath with any serious exercise.

Robin was an intelligent woman, energetic almost to the point of being high-strung. She worked her way up to a respected position as a marketing consultant before meeting Joe. Once the kids came along she worked less, but still volunteered her time for a number of charities. Smoking seemed to help her keep up with herself.

After their third child mysteriously died at eight months of age, she had begun to seriously suspect tobacco. There was no known connection, but.... Everywhere she looked there was more new information about the consequences of smoking. Then her father had developed lung cancer and died. She simply lost her taste for smoking after that, and after some counseling from Robert had stopped shortly after a hiking holiday in South America.

Later she'd tell people, "Sure, I just quit, just like that." Actually, people don't usually suddenly end their compulsive behaviors or addictions. Instead they edge towards stopping, over a period of months or years, and finally make the move.

Whether the problem is overeating, alcohol, gambling, nicotine, or any other compulsive behavior, change is a process that takes preparation, effort, and follow-through. Relapse to smoking again is common. Only those who persist and quit repeatedly, learning from past mistakes (five times is average), ultimately live smoke-free.

Robin's success at overcoming smoking provides a good example of how any out-of-control, high-flying habit can be brought down to a safe landing. Like any adult must, she went through six 'stages of change' on her journey from compulsion to control, from slavery to freedom.* (It's important to note these stages may not apply to adolescents.)

Pre-contemplation . . .
    Contemplation . . .
        Preparation . . .
            Action! . . . . .
                Maintenance . . .Termination.

    I. Pre-contemplation . . .not even considering change
   II. Contemplation . . . . .thinking about it
  III. Preparation . . . . .getting ready to stop
  IV. Action! . . . . .actually stopping
   V. Maintenance . . . . . . .staying stopped
  VI. Termination . . . . .will never start again

I. PRE-CONTEMPLATION

A nagging cough had first prompted Robin to consult Dr. Borenot. She usually ignored nagging of any kind, but these were deep, chest-heaving spasms that brought forth tears from her eyes, and thick purulent phlegm from the darkest corners of her lungs.

After a chest x-ray confirmed the clinical impression of severe pneumonia, Robin declined hospitalization but gratefully accepted antibiotics for what she called her "cold." Dr. Borenot offered her information on tobacco and health. "No thanks, Doc," she wheezed, "I don't need to quit."

Robin shrugged off her doctor's advice. Her relatives were all practically immortal, she reassured him. Her ninety-five year old grandmother, for example, had consumed a couple of cigars and a pack of cigarettes daily beginning in her

* Based on the work of James O. Prochaska, John C. Norcross, and Carlo C. DiClemente. See "Recommended Books."

early adolescence. Though getting a bit slower off the start as she aged, she could still out-pace an average racehorse.

At any given time no more than 10% to 15% of smokers are actively preparing to quit. Most are in the *precontemplation* and *contemplation* stages of the process.

In general, "pre-contemplators" don't know how harmful smoking really is nor do they accept the fact that they will be personally affected. During the precontemplation stage, female smokers may not know — or want to know — that smoking is one cause of thinning of the bones (osteoporosis) which often leads to broken hips and wrists. Males in that stage are often surprised to learn that smoking eventually contributes to impotence.

> The pre-contemplator's mission, should he or she choose to accept it, is simply to acknowledge that there is hope, and to get the facts straight.

II. CONTEMPLATION

Not long after Robin's pneumonia resolved, her chain-smoking father was diagnosed with inoperable lung cancer. Robin learned the hard way that 90% of all lung cancers and a large percentage of other fatal diseases in North America are caused by cigarette smoking. "That can't be true," she said, but wondered aloud why governments so freely permit the sale and promotion of tobacco.

"I'll quit eventually," Robin told Robert. *"It's just not a very good time right now. I'm too stressed already."* She was quite right. Some people do stop smoking immediately upon making the connection between tobacco and disease. The urge to quit might soon follow the realization that tobacco kills them and people around them. But long-term commitments made on the spur of an emotional moment are built on

a fragile foundation and may not endure.

Robin's attitude changed slightly with her third pregnancy. *"I don't really want to stop,"* she admitted, *"but I'd like to want to quit."* It's natural to have a degree of ambivalence about anything in life, and smoking is no exception. Seventy percent of smokers say they would like to quit, but 100% of them smoke.

Over the next few months Robin saw Dr. Borenot for regular prenatal visits, and in connection with her father's illness. She was surprised to learn that while not every smoker will suffer from cancer, a heart attack, or a stroke, other consequences of smoking are unavoidable. She hadn't known that smoking harms the blood vessels causing circulation problems (impotence, cold feet, painful legs when walking), decreases the power of the immune system to fight infection, and destroys lung tissue.

Her father passed away before seeing his third grandchild. Joey was born three months later without incident and thrived until the age of eight months, when he mysteriously died in his sleep. Sudden infant death syndrome, apparently. No words could describe Robin and Joe's grieving.

Robin began to have real qualms about smoking and the tobacco industry's position that tobacco was perfectly harmless. She and Joe even quarreled about it, until they eventually agreed to disagree.

The task for those in the contemplation stage, should they choose to accept it, is to learn about the benefits and techniques of quitting.

III. PREPARATION

People often decide to change their self-destructive behavior when they begin to feel the consequences. Perhaps some internal voice or wisdom insists that life is too precious an opportunity to waste.

Some months after her son died, Robin went hiking in South America. Whether from the weight of her grieving or due to the lack of oxygen at high altitude, she could barely keep up with others almost twice her age. It was difficult for her to breathe, let alone to smoke.

"I've got to quit," Robin told Robert upon her return. "Smoking is killing me."

Robin then monitored her smoking for a couple of weeks and made plans to avoid or change her 'triggers.' Because she felt that altering her routine would make stopping easier, she switched brands, placed her cigarettes upside down in the pack, began using matches instead of a lighter, and smoked in different places and at different times than usual.

In preparation for quitting she also asked her friends and family to help her. She took up walking more, and reorganized her life to minimize stress. Finally she set a target date, the day on which she would stop smoking forever. Joe mostly pretended this all wasn't happening but didn't actively discourage her.

The task in the preparation stage, after having chosen to accept change, is to get ready to make it happen.

IV. ACTION!

Robin smoked her last cigarette the evening before her target date. The next morning she slapped on a nicotine patch and dropped two handfuls of money into a big glass jar — her first day of savings from not smoking. She felt no desire to light up while driving in her freshly-cleaned car. The change was unfamiliar and even a bit scary.

She experienced an unusual sense of power and calm over the next few days, and was pleasantly surprised that controlled nicotine withdrawal was quite manageable. She avoided or changed her major smoking triggers, according to plan. When the urge to smoke was strong, she'd put on her new walking shoes and enjoy a brisk stroll.

Even in those early days of freedom she felt her body recovering. The occasional discomfort of quitting was balanced by relief at finally having tackled her problem.

The task in the action stage is simply to stop smoking.

V. MAINTENANCE

During the next three months Robin worked hard at maintaining her smoke-free status. She carefully avoided the triggers and cues that she'd identified during the preparation stage, and she kept herself busy. Far from being burdened by the task, she had more energy available for things she'd always wanted to do.

Robin used nicotine replacement faithfully and got more exercise. To prevent weight gain she ate well but wisely. She could breathe easier, didn't cough as much, and felt extremely proud of herself.

After two weeks Robin almost fell off the non-smoking wagon, when she'd had a bit much to drink at a company celebration. Everybody else is smoking, she thought, and just one won't hurt, will it? I've been so good, and I deserve a break. Just one.

Fortunately during her preparation phase she'd read three helpful *"Rules of Relapse,"* and was able to follow them. Instead of bumming a cigarette she excused herself and sought out a vending machine from which to buy a pack. On the way she almost changed her mind, but soon had a lit cigarette in her hand. Even though the smoke tasted strangely awful, the nicotine felt good.

Throwing the rest of the pack away immediately was not so easy. "Why waste perfectly good cigarettes?" she reasoned. "Perfectly good cigarettes?" she reasoned again, and tossed the pack down a sewer. On the way back to the party she felt much stronger, slightly sobered and better able to handle future temptations.

Relapse can lead to a sense of failure and the belief that one will never be able to quit. If one does slip, negative thoughts can drag one right back down the mountain. The path to the summit of success is rocky and difficult enough without the burden of negative thinking. Travel light.

The most sure-footed way to succeed without setbacks is to take one confident step at a time. Slips may happen; learn from them.

The tasks in the maintenance stage include consistently avoiding triggers, and using new ways of coping with stress. Also, celebrating personal power and rejoicing!

VI. TERMINATION

After three years Robin knew that she'd never smoke another cigarette. In the meantime she had relapsed twice but not without learning more about herself and nicotine addiction. After each relapse she followed through by quitting once more, applying what she'd learned. Several battles later, she'd finally won the war.

Finally, Robin had benefited so much from being smoke-free that she could hardly remember why she ever smoked.

There is really no task in the termination phase, except being a smoke-free example to others and offering whatever help is possible.

* * * * *

Robin finished her coffee and walked back to the elevators, away from the sight of the smoking patients. She left the craving somewhere about the third floor, and continued on upwards to check on Joe in the Intensive Care Unit.

THE RULES OF RELAPSE*

1. Never ask for a cigarette or accept one that is offered to you. *Buy your own.*
2. Never buy cigarettes in the place where you are about to relapse. *Go somewhere else!*
3. After smoking just one cigarette, *immediately destroy the rest of the pack you just bought.*

*After Klesges R, DeBon M. *How Women Can Finally Stop Smoking*. Alameda: Hunter House, 1994: p. 133. See "Recommended Books."

12

There Is A Difference

There is very little difference between men and women in space.
— *Helen Sharman*

...except where nicotine is concerned.
— *Simon Bryant*

March 17th

"*H*E WHAT?"

"Joe had a cardiac arrest on the operating table," Robin repeated. Robert was amazed. Those mysterious memos, the burglary of his office, and now this. What next?

"Is he all right?"

"Yes, he's doing fine. He'll be transferred out of the ICU into a private room later today. He said he'd like to see you as soon as possible."

"I'll be there this afternoon."

At the hospital a discreet attendant ushered Robert in to Joe's suite, past a wall of blossoms and foliage. It appeared that the best part of a flower shop had been transplanted to his lounge.

Joe was awake and resting comfortably in an easy chair, taking in the spring sunshine and the view of the city from the tenth floor. His silk dressing gown rippled light as he rose to welcome Robert with a firm handshake.

"It's all good news, Robert," Joe announced after they'd exchanged greetings. "They say they got it all." That probably meant that Joe was completely cured.

"Fantastic, Joe. And you haven't smoked in over two weeks. I'm not sure the time on a respirator counts, but congratulations for the others!"

Joe smiled crookedly. "Thanks. Does this mean I've made it over the hump?"

"Let's hope so!" On the other hand, Robert thought, in one survey 40% of heart attack victims were smoking again within two weeks of leaving hospital, as were more than half those who had had their voice box or part of a lung removed.

"But keep your guard up. By the way, Joe, there's something I wanted to ask you about."

In Robert's pocket was the photocopied document that Joe must have dropped in his office. At first Robert had been uncertain what to do with the evidence, as he thought of it. His first impulse had been to return it to Joe at their next meeting, but then after the burglary he'd placed the paper in his safety deposit box.

Robert was just about to produce the memo when Robin arrived with the children. She greeted Robert warmly and then sat on the edge of Joe's chair, throwing an arm around his shoulders and holding him close.

"Isn't he great?" she asked Robert. "My hero." After checking on their father the kids busied themselves demolishing a vulnerable fruit basket and sampling the offerings on the cable television.

During some chat about the favorable diagnosis and what a fine day it was, Joe abruptly spoke of his experience during the surgery.

"You know, I almost died on that operating table," he said. "I don't know what you think of this, Robert, but I swear I left my body for awhile. I could hear and see the doctors reacting. Maybe they just put too much joy-juice in my intravenous, or something."

"Or maybe you really did leave your body," Robin proposed. "I've heard stories about that."

"And then I met Elvis on Mars," Joe quipped, "and…." He paused, thoughtful, before continuing in a more serious tone. "It was really quite an uncanny experience. It felt *real*. I can't get it out of my head. Some figures appeared and asked me something." Then he lapsed into reflective silence.

"Did they ask you something like *what have you learned, and what have you done for other people?*" Robert enquired.

"What? How did you know that?" Joe asked, startled. He looked at Robin. "Did you…"

"No, I didn't tell him anything, my dear," she said.

"Many people have reported being asked that kind of question during near-death experiences," Robert reassured him, with good effect.

"Really? What's that all about?" Joe asked.

"I've no idea. Maybe it's our conscience, or perhaps we just ask ourselves those questions. How do you feel about it now, Joe?"

"About what?" he asked.

"About what you've done with your life, and what you've learned," Robin prompted.

"I'm not sure. It's a wonderful shock to be here today, and to have such good news. Look at me. I've got my loving wife and kids right here, I've got my health back. What more could I ask for? I feel like I really did die and now I'm in a heaven I don't deserve."

Robert smiled uncontrollably and Robin blinked hard.

"And you've got more money than is good for you," Robin joked. "But don't worry, I know what to do with that. And it's not what you think."

Robert was intrigued by the near-death experience, but Joe seemed unwilling to say much more about it. The talk turned briefly to the heart made of muscle, and away from the heart of the soul.

"One of the surgeons told me he was reaching for a scalpel to slice open my ribs and stick his hand in. He was going to grab my heart and pump it for me!" Joe said. "I told him that was mighty kind of him. With friends like that, how can a guy up and die?"

The children returned from their exploration of the suite, and Robert felt himself an intruder into the family's time.

"I really should be going now," he said. He still had Joe's memos and was very curious about the upcoming government tobacco hearings, but those things could wait.

On the other hand... "By the way, Joe, are you still scheduled to testify at those hearings?" Robert asked offhandedly. Joe shrugged with a dismissive gesture.

"I'll burn that bridge when I come to it," he said enigmatically, leaving no doubt that he didn't wish to discuss the matter. It was time to go, and Robert said as much.

"Oh, just a minute. Here." Robin pulled a small brown envelope from her bag and passed it to Robert "The *women and smoking* assignment" she said. "On tape. Joe and I sort of collaborated on it."

Robert smiled. "Thanks. I look forward to hearing it later." He slipped the tape into his jacket pocket, where his hand met the envelope that he'd wanted to give to Joe. Perhaps he could pass it over in the guise of a get-well card? Better to wait, he thought. There'd be a chance to talk about it eventually, when Joe could meet him in the office again.

There was more to be said but none of them had the words just then. "I'm sure glad you made it through that surgery, Joe," Robert finally managed.

"Amen, Doc."

Robert completed his good-byes and emerged from the hospital into the light of a fine spring evening. Trees were budding and flowers were pushing up from the dirt. The air was fresh, and clean. It was good to be alive.

On his way home Robert slipped Robin and Joe's cassette into the tape deck in his car. He could make out a general kitchen ruckus, with dishes clattering and the kids saying something about playing in the park. Joe was talking about going to the hospital, and Robin announced that the coffee was ready.

Robert: A few things to wrap up… talk with the lawyers…

Robin: … that assignment about women and smoking?

He: … no time.

She: Just tell him what you know, honey. Here, I'm even recording this conversation for you. Just keep talking.

He: What? That machine is turned on?

She: Sure. We'll just give him the tape, if it turns out. Why not try something different?

He: I don't know. I haven't collected much material… prepare a little handout or something.

She: Aww, come on, Joe. Have some fun with it. Just talk about what you know, and what you're feeling. Did you know that women get more support for quitting from others than men do? I think it's because they share their feelings more. Just start talking. Otherwise you're never going to get this assignment done.

He: Okay, here goes. Right off the top of my head, Robert, I know that women's bodies break down nicotine a bit slower than men's bodies do. They tend to get more severe withdrawal symptoms, especially if they try and quit before rather than after their menstrual cycle.

She: That's right. Boy, you guys get all the breaks. No childbirth, and easier nicotine withdrawal. And we have to deal with all the brainwashing marketing, too.

He: What are you talking about?

She: You know, Joe. Stuff like the Lucky Stroke campaign and that slogan, "Reach for a Luckie instead of a sweet" Shame on you guys, preying on our insecurities about appearance. And then, "You've come a long way, baby." Who thought that one up, I wonder?

He: Virginia's Limbs? That was one of the most effective advertisements ever.

She: So you acknowledge that women are targeted by tobacco advertising?

He: Sure, but no more than any other group.

She: Right. And don't women tend to be more concerned about the possibility of weight gain after quitting?

He: An average of six pounds for men, and nine pounds for women. Good reason to keep smoking, right?

She: Bite your tongue! Young women are more likely than young men to believe that smoking controls weight. And that's just not true.

He: No, but it probably sells a lot of cigarettes.

She: Now you're making nonsense. You know, you're acting kind of cynical since you quit smoking.

He: Go figure. These patches are great, but I'm still going under the knife in a couple of days. Assuming I survive that, then I have to testify, under oath for God's sake, before some hostile panel of inquiring laser-minds at that government hearing.

She: You're doing great, honey. I'm so proud of you.

He: Thanks. I love you, you know.

She: It's mutual. So let's finish this assignment and do something about it.

He: I'm done.

She: No way, Joe. Is that all you have to say about women and smoking?

He: What more is there to say?

She: What about oral contraceptives? It isn't fair. There's no pill for men, but women who smoke and take the pill increase their risk of getting fatal blood clots. And I don't see a whole lot of women high up in the tobacco industry.

He: Hey, we've got Margaret Thatcher as a consultant.

She: I believe she said that being in politics taught her that men are neither reasoned nor reasonable. But that's besides the point. Aren't you going to mention that women tend to smoke to reduce negative emotions like stress and frustration, whereas men seem to smoke for stimulation?

He: Slipped my mind, I guess.

She: You see, we women have to smoke so we can put up with you guys.

He: Hey, play fair.

She: Okay. You also forgot to mention that smoking reduces circulating estrogen, leading to thinning of the bones and hip fractures. So insensitive!

(There was the sound of feet, laughter and scraping chairs as if somebody was being chased around the kitchen table, followed by Joe's somewhat breathless voice.)

He: And now to continue with our special report on smoking and women's health brought to you direct and live from the Hamel kitchen, featuring our distinguished expert Robin Hamel.

She: Joe, I'd just like to thank you for this opportunity to say a few words to the public on behalf of women everywhere. We've been exploited by the cynical manipulations of tobacco companies long enough. Far from liberating us, the tobacco industry seeks to enslave women through nicotine addiction and deviously-designed advertising campaigns that prey on our insecurities. In addition to the usual risks associated with smoking such as heart disease, stroke, emphysema, cancer, and impaired immune function, women suffer reduced fertility, earlier menopause, and possibly a greater dependency on nicotine. As if child-bearing weren't unfair enough, women must also bear the burden of responsibility for damage to their babies caused by smoking during pregnancy. Studies have shown that... oh, no.

He: It's okay, honey. I'm with you. I hear you.

There was a click and then silence.

Robert felt drained by the day. He stopped at a restaurant near his home, and completed the chart entry while waiting for his supper.

* * * * *

Joe survived his successful operation, and hasn't smoked in 17 days. He had a fascinating near-death experience during the surgery last week, complete with guiding spirits giving him a grilling about his life's priorities. I'm not sure what to make of it. It will be interesting to see what he does!

I'm learning a great deal from Joe, and Robin. Over the past few weeks he's reminded me that there's more to smoking than simply nicotine addiction.

Quitting is an act of creation, of new possibilities. It's some- thing that happens between individuals and their goals, dreams, and environments. When they really stop smoking, people change their lives and their futures.

Joe is almost into the maintenance stage now. The next few months will be a test, in many ways.

Robin is a solid support for Joe. She obviously feels very strongly about not smoking and I wonder how they managed to reconcile that difference over the past few years.

They are a couple of strong personalities, with great poten- tial for good.

13

Fat in The Fire

*When you come right down to it all you
have is yourself. The sun is a thousand
rays in your belly. All the rest is nothing.*

— Picasso

March 31st

TWO WEEKS LATER Joe breezed into Robert's office looking relaxed and composed. He hung up his expensive leather jacket and removed his sunglasses, tucking them in his shirt pocket before sitting down.

They exchanged warm greetings and news but Joe avoided meeting Robert's gaze for very long.

"How's Joe?" Robert asked.

"Winning. Still not smoking," Joe said. Robert couldn't quite put his finger on it, but there was something different about Joe's manner and bearing. But people often took a few steps backward every so often. Rather than "three steps forward, two backward," Robert preferred to think of it as taking a run at the next obstacle.

Joe casually took out a fresh pack of cigarettes and tossed it onto the low table. Robert made no comment, waiting.

"I was 'medically unfit' to attend those government hearings," Joe said.

Robert figured that Joe could easily have appeared, and perhaps spoken the truth. Nobody else had. To a man — and no women testified — the tobacco industry executives had simply denied that tobacco had any ill effects or that nicotine was addictive. There'd been murmurs about charging them all with perjury.

"It would have been quite stressful for you to be on the stand," Robert offered. Joe chuckled and smiled like a cat who'd just discovered that he had a tenth life after all.

"Indeed. I'm a hero at work now, by the way. Living proof that all cancers aren't due to smoking. Mine wasn't."

"And what does that say about the 90% of lung cancers that *are* caused by tobacco smoke?" Robert asked.

"Nothing," said Joe. "But they've bankrolled the *Joe K. Hamel Cancer Survival Foundation* to sponsor research into rare cancers, anyway." Robert didn't know what to say.

"I pushed for it, you know, as part of my retirement package. The board loved it."

"That's wonderful, Joe," Robert said. "Every little bit helps. You must be proud. So you're planning to retire?"

Joe stared directly at Robert.

"Yeah. The company's been very generous with me. I might as well enjoy what's left of my life."

What a change, thought Robert. *This really isn't the same fellow I last saw in hospital.*

"And what's on your agenda now, Joe?"

"My weight, I guess" Joe said, glancing down at and patting his moderate gut. "I gained five pounds right after quitting, lost ten in the hospital, and now it's finding me again. I think I've gained about six in the past couple of weeks."

"That rapid a fluctuation is probably because of water retention and loss," Robert explained. "Nicotine is a mild diuretic, so it's not uncommon to gain three or four pounds right after quitting. That doesn't continue, of course."

Robert rummaged in his files and murmured to himself. "Let's see now. Weight control. Ah, here it is." He presented Joe with a menu card.

	The Calorie Cafe
Appetizer	Why weight?
Soup	How smoking affects body weight.
Salad	How quitting affects body weight.
Main course	How activity affects body weight.
Desert	Real chocolate cigars.
	"Correct" smoking only, please.

"Imagine that you're dining at the Calorie Café, Joe. It's a very classy joint, incidentally."

"Quite my style, then?" Joe asked, quite amused.

"Of course, Monsieur. There's a valet to park your car and a uniformed doorman. The maître d' asks *why weight, Sir?* as he immediately shows you to your favorite seat. It's a good question. Despite what many people think, weight gain or loss doesn't depend on how much you eat.

"In the center of the restaurant there's a peculiar sort of fountain. A trickle of water falls into a large glass container, about one-half full, that is drained by a faucet set near the bottom. The two flows are perfectly matched so that the water level in the container never changes.

THE LAW OF BODY WEIGHT

Calories in
+/- Calories out
= change in weight

Calories in:

food item	calories
soft drink, 10 oz	105
cheesecake, 1 slice	260
butter, 1 tsp	50
fried chicken, 4 oz	325
beefsteak, 4 oz	350
apple	76
milk, whole, 1 cup	153
milk, skim, 1 cup	84

Calories out:

activity	cal/hr
walking, 3 mph	264
walking, 4 mph	396
rowing	420
cycling, 9 mph	400
typing (electric)	108
piano playing	160
running fast	936

"The human body is much like that fountain, Joe. The inflow represents any food or drink consumed, while the outflow represents calories burned off through physical activity. The amount of water in the reservoir is body weight. If the two flows are equal, the water level won't change. On the other hand, if more water pours in than runs out, it will accumulate in the container."

Joe drew the obvious conclusion. "In other words, to gain weight a person must eat more calories than he or she burns off?" he asked.

"Exactly."

"But it's not that simple," said Joe. "Some people always feel hungry, even with a full stomach. Or maybe they absorb almost every calorie they eat."

"Sure there are individual differences," Robert agreed. "But it's impossible to gain weight without consuming more calories than you expend. That's simply a law of physics. Food for thought, isn't it?"

Joe wasn't so easily satisfied. He sat with his arms folded, waiting for the next course. "Okay," he consented, "but how does smoking fit in?"

"Smoking makes the body burn about 100 calories extra, every day. That means smokers can avoid a 19-minute walk daily and eat the same amount as a non-smoker, without affecting their weight."

Joe looked a bit uncertain.

"Think of the fountain, Joe. Smoking is like opening the drain a bit. Close it an equal amount by avoiding the walk, and the water level won't change from one day to another."

Joe nodded. "You mean a smoker can eat only 100 calories a day more than a non-smoker, without gaining weight?" he asked, still somewhat sceptical.

"That's about right, Joe. And one hundred calories means

just one medium canned peach, or two teaspoons of butter. So a tiny snack can cancel out the total calorie-burning effect of smoking. You see, the balance between food in and energy out makes far more difference to a person's weight than smoking does.

"Smoking doesn't prevent weight gain," Robert emphasized. "One study of women smokers showed that over a period of ten years, during which they continued to smoke, 10% gained between 17 and 28 pounds, and 5% gained more than 28 pounds."

"But what about quitting?" Joe asked, glancing at his menu. "Why do people balloon when they stop smoking?"

"They don't really. You might hear about the occasional ex-smoker gaining forty pounds or so after quitting, but that's very unusual. On the other hand it's very usual to hear about and remember the unusual."

"Say again?" Joe asked.

"The boring truth is that the average weight gain after quitting smoking is about six pounds in men and nine pounds in women. Those who smoke weigh on average about eight pounds less than non-smokers, and regain just enough weight after quitting to make up the difference."

"Where does the weight *come* from after you quit smoking, though?"

"About one-third can be blamed on the body burning less calories," Robert responded, "and the other two-thirds on the body eating more, usually high carbohydrate snacks. Remember, if you gain weight it's because you're taking in more calories than you're burning off."

"Some bodies must leave their owners sleeping and raid the refrigerator every night," suggested Joe. "Now what I'd like to know is, how can I avoid gaining weight?"

"That's easy. Eat reasonably and be physically active."

"That's it?"

Robert began his explanation of "caloric balance" once again, this time using a different example that would include the role of dietary fat.

"Imagine that you're an automobile, Joe. At the gas station your driver asks for twenty gallons of gas. There's only room for ten gallons in the tank, so the obliging attendant attaches an extra ten-gallon container to your back bumper, and fills it up. Your rear end loses its sleek appearance, but you can still move around."

"I beg your pardon? What was that about my rear end?"

"Figuratively speaking, Joe. Imagine that the filling station scene is repeated many times, until you're loaded down with an assortment of gas-filled containers. Your original shape is completely hidden and your suspension is groaning under the strain. It's a disaster waiting to happen."

Joe was laughing at this particular example.

"Finally an attendant at one gas station insists that you've got too much gas on board. 'You're filling up with more than you're using up,' he says. 'I've seen it before. You've got to move, and not fill up so often. Don't use the fat-fuel, either.'"

"What's wrong with fat-fuel?" Joe demanded. "There's nothing quite like a greasy burger with fries and onion rings."

"Food contains fat, carbohydrate, and protein. The body automatically burns off about 10% of the calories that you've eaten in the form of carbohydrates and proteins, but calories consumed in the form of fat just get absorbed and stored. So for the same amount of calories, a person will gain less weight from carbohydrates and proteins than from fat."

Robert finished his explanation by emphasizing the importance of activity.

"Physical activity is a superb way to control weight. Exercising vigorously for twenty to thirty minutes, three times weekly, is enough to compensate for moderate over-eating. Do you realize that stenographers gained an average of ten pounds when electric typewriters replaced manual ones? The key to controlling weight is simply to move, and to build up some muscle if you so choose."

"Eat more without gaining weight?" Joe asked. "That's surely impossible."

"Well, the best example I can think of involved a group of 50–80 year olds in a weight-training program. I have the paper here somewhere, if you want."

Joe shook his head, and Robert continued.

"Their body fat decreased by just 3%, but their strength increased by anywhere from 24% to 92%. Their metabolism speeded up by 8%, and when that was added to the extra calories they burned up by exercising, they were able to eat 800 calories more per day without gaining any weight."

"You mean they got stronger, ate more, and lost weight?"

"That's right, Joe. Older folk, pumping iron. Isn't it great? And there are other benefits of exercise," Robert said. "Improved sleep, better sense of self-control and self-esteem, increased resistance to disease, and last but not least, a greater chance of quitting smoking."

"I still don't think it's possible to quit smoking without gaining at least *some* weight," Joe objected.

Robert didn't answer him. He silently rummaged among his files, finding two articles which he then passed to Joe. "Here," he finally spoke, "You can read these sometime and judge for yourself." Joe glanced at the papers, then carefully filed them in his briefcase.

"Rigid beliefs can create problems, Joe," Robert gently suggested. "There's beliefs, and then there's the facts. They aren't always the same."

Joe listened attentively.

"I want to make a point about beliefs, but first let's wrap up the weight gain issue. There's a few more factors to consider than I mentioned. Firstly, smoking is an appetite suppressant, an effect likely mediated through the release of the chemicals serotonin and dopamine in the brain. Secondly, nicotine can stimulate your adrenal glands to produce adrenaline, which causes your liver to release glucose into the blood and fat cells to release stored fatty acids. This also reduces appetite. Thirdly, when you smoke and lose weight your body may compensate by trying harder to store energy in fat cells, which involves an increase in the amount and activity of certain enzymes, notably adipose tissue lipoprotein lipase (AT-LPL). After quitting, this increased activity can persist and partly explains the tendency to gain weight."

Joe was vindicated. "Aha! So there's more to the weight gain story than you mentioned! I thought so."

"The bottom line doesn't change, Joe. I mentioned those details about the physiology of weight gain because I didn't want you going off and hearing them somewhere else, and thinking I'd misled you. The solution to preventing or dealing with weight gain is increased activity, low fat diet, and building and using muscle. Exercise itself can be an appetite suppressant, and a wise choice of food and drink can go a long way towards controlling weight.

"Now, here's the point I wanted to make about beliefs. Consider the statements, 'I eat hardly anything but I can't lose weight' or 'I can't quit smoking.' Are they really valid? If we admit someone to hospital for a couple of weeks and control their intake, they lose weight. Of all the people who have ever smoked, half have already quit. So stopping smoking and losing weight are both very possible.

"It's tough to be really being honest with yourself," he added, pausing to watch Joe's reaction. Silence and eye contact suggested an opportunity.

"Change actually begins *before* any action takes place. When a person starts to believe that change is possible, then it's really already happened. I'm not saying that altering a lifestyle is easy. I'm just suggesting that belief is the key. You've got to have faith in yourself and your ability to change," Robert suggested.

Good. Joe nodded and seemed to have absorbed that essential idea. Robert looked down and noticed the unopened cigarette pack on the table. He'd been so absorbed in lecturing, he'd forgotten all about it.

"What's that about, Joe?" he asked, pointing.

"I thought you were never going to ask," said Joe, smiling and picking up the pack. He stripped off the cellophane cover, broke the seal, and fished his lighter from his pocket. Robert stared.

"This is my latest aid to quitting," said Joe. Inside the package were twenty little scrolls of paper. He produced one, unrolled it, and read out "Impotence." A flick of the lighter, and the paper burned. The next scroll was a five-dollar bill, which left a fine ash with the printing still visible. "A waste of money," Joe said before burning three more scrolls: "Cough," "Cancer," and "Effects on Others."

"That's a fantastic idea," said Robert. Joe was way ahead, after all. So much for lecturing him about beliefs!

"Thanks. I go through one of these special packs from time to time. It helps. Now how about those chocolate cigars I saw on the menu?" Joe asked.

"Oh, pardon me," Robert joked. "Would monsieur care for a chocolate cigar? About 100 calories each. Eating ten a day in addition to the body's requirements will increase your body fat by a hundred pounds after one year, more or less. Incidentally, that's how much weight one would have to gain to equal the health risk of smoking one pack daily."

"Not today, thanks," Joe said.

Joe said he had some things to do next week, so they agreed to meet in two week's time. They said their good-byes after a short discussion about the nicotine replacement Joe was using, and the "decisional balance" assignment.

It was only after Joe had left that Robert realized he hadn't returned the misplaced memo.

* * * * *

In his record for the day Robert wrote:

Joe remains smoke free, and appears optimistic about the future. Nicotine replacement seems to be controlling his withdrawal symptoms.

He was a bit reserved today. I'm not sure what's going on. I feel as though he is watching me, as though he doesn't fully trust me. Perhaps he shouldn't; I completely forgot to give him back the papers I assume he left here.

I lapsed into lecturing him about beliefs today, but he completely outsmarted me; he's way ahead, and has devised a clever 'cigarette pack' of reasons not to smoke.

We'll meet again in two weeks.

For next session: advertising?

14

Seeing Through Smoke

We are never deceived; we deceive ourselves.
— Goethe

April 14th

I T WAS FULL-BLOWN SPRING, and anything that was
going to grow that year had already declared itself. Or so
Robert thought as he walked to the office for a follow-up session with Joe. The man had stopped smoking, and was free
of his illness. Free as a bird. The margins of the excised tissue were free of any tumor. Free and clear. Smoke-free.

This would be their second-to-last appointment. I'll miss
these regular meetings, thought Robert.

He placed Joe's envelope on the desk where he wouldn't
forget it. He'd had a nagging impulse to discuss the memos
with others, because they appeared to contradict the tobacco
industry's public stance. They would surely be of interest to
journalists and perhaps law enforcement officials. On the
other hand, Robert had an ethical obligation to maintain his
patients' confidentiality.

It would have been one thing to find such a document in
the street, or discreetly slipped into one's mailbox. It was
quite another to obtain it by accident from a client. But then
perhaps it hadn't been an accident?

Joe pulled up outside Robert's office a few fashionable
minutes late, riding a large and loud motorcycle. He parked
the bike and sauntered into Robert's office, tanned and smiling, and swung himself into the familiar chair.

"How's it going, on day 44?" Robert inquired.

"Not so bad, Doc," replied Joe. "I haven't smoked at all
yet, and I intend not to."

"Congratulations. You must be doing something right.
The first few weeks are tough ones. "

"Thanks. I guess all it takes is a cancer, four months of
weekly therapy, and a wife who's totally committed to the
no-smoking cause."

"And motivation, preparation, and perseverance, Joe. So how are you managing? Any serious temptations or cravings, or 'near misses'?"

"Yeah. It's tough sometimes but I'm not a quitter," Joe said. *Clever.* There was a hint of their old relationship in the chuckle they shared at the double meaning. "I keep that 'balance of power' thing handy. You know, that last assignment from before the surgery," he added.

"Of course. Do you find that helpful?" Robert asked.

"For sure. I like to see the big picture, at a glance." Joe produced a folded photocopy of the assignment from his wallet, and smoothed it out on the table.

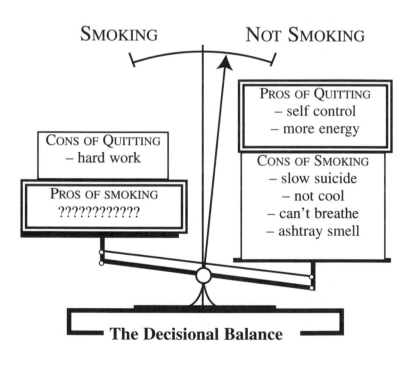

The Decisional Balance

"That looks pretty convincing, Joe. I can see that the scales are tipped towards not smoking. Tell me though, are there any times when you feel strong cravings to smoke?"

"You must mean from the moment I wake up until when I finally fall sleep?"

Robert laughed. "Okay. But when are the worst times?"

"Well, I can handle the after-meal situations. I often just take my coffee in a travel mug like you suggested, and go for a walk. I can handle the phone call urges. I've put a treadmill by the phone at home, and I just stroll along while talking. Robin calls it 'walking the talk.' But you know what really gets to me? Advertising."

"Advertising? Nobody's ever told me that advertisements make them want to smoke, quite like that," Robert said.

"Maybe not, but I'll be doing fine, driving down the road smoke-free as you please. Then I might see a huge smoking billboard and I just want to light up all over again. Or I open a magazine and see a cigarette advertisement, and it drives me crazy. They're always in my face."

"I guess that's how advertising is supposed to work," Robert said, "but I've never heard of anybody having such a strong reaction to it."

"You're not sure how advertising works, Doc? I'll tell you. Years ago, I used to dream up those ads myself.

"The idea is to pair up a cigarette brand name or logo with something appealing, such as car racing, sexy women, handsome guys, a symphony orchestra, or whatever. It all depends who the target audience is. Now, it's just human nature to make a connection between cigarettes and the excitement of racing, after a tobacco-sponsored Formula One car flashes across your television screen for the five-hundredth time. You can't help it. Eventually the bait is linked with smoking in the audience's mind."

"It's that simple?" Robert asked.

"You bet. Of course car racing has nothing whatsoever to do with smoking, or vice versa. It's just a question of associating the two often enough. Now this has really backfired on me. Like I said, I used to do creative advertising work. While smoking, of course. Later on I'd listen to hired hands trying to sell me their ad ideas, while smoking. I'd always have a smoke while reviewing advertising reports and focus sessions. Now advertising is a *trigger*, for me."

Robert couldn't help thinking of the tobacco industry's position that advertising was only intended to promote switching brands, and not at all to get people smoking in the first place.

"I don't suppose there's any way you can avoid the advertising," said Robert. "What about changing it?"

"Changing advertising? I can't do that," said Joe.

"What about hijacking it, then?"

HOW TO HIJACK TOBACCO ADVERTISING

1. Choose your "favorite" tobacco advertisement from any magazine.
2. With a few strokes of colored pencil or correction fluid, remove any cigarettes or reference to them.
3. Glue a photograph of your smiling face into the finest spot of the advertisement, and post your fantasy-creation somewhere you'll see it frequently.
4. Make a list of small steps you can take towards realizing your dreams, and post it beside the modified advertisement. Every day, try to take even a tiny step in the right direction. Smoking has nothing to do with it.

"Hijacking advertising? I don't get it."

Robert searched among the clutter on his desk, retrieving a paper that he passed to Joe. "Here, tell me what you think of this. You can't avoid advertising, so why not use it to your advantage?" Joe considered the directions.

"No, I don't think that would be very effective at all," he said. "It wouldn't work with "lifestyle" ads where nobody is shown smoking. The psychology of those ads is very subtle, but they work. And we sponsor sport and cultural events. You couldn't use this approach with that kind of advertising. It wouldn't work with branded merchandise, either."

"You mean like clothing with cigarette advertising on it?" Robert asked. "I once met a fellow wearing a picture of the Kamel dragster on his T-shirt. Smoke poured from the massive rear tires, Joe, right over his heart. He'd picked it up for free at the drag races, where the Kamel-car smoked the competition. Not surprising, considering the money invested. What do you think this fellow had to say about it?"

"I don't know. Kamels are a drag? I wouldn't walk a quarter-mile for a Kamel? I don't know, what did he say?"

"*I can't imagine where they get the money.* He figured it out, though. Quit smoking a month later, too."

"You're good at what you do, Robert," Joe said.

"Thanks. And so were you."

Joe took Robert's compliment in an unintended way.

"Hey, that's not fair. Look, I admit I've made some mistakes, but I'm out of the tobacco business now."

Robert apologized. He'd accidentally struck a nerve. Joe insisted on explaining himself.

"You say I was good at what I did. I may have screwed up badly in my choice of career, Robert, but I'm raising two kids I'm proud of. And as far as tobacco and Mr. Joe Hamel are concerned, the game isn't over yet.

"I was a young man with a business degree and powerful ambitions. I took the best offer going, joined a tobacco company and crawled my way up the ladder. Life was comfortable, the pay was exceptional, and all was well.

"You know, I used to think I might become the president of the company. Imagine that. I'm sure glad I didn't. At one point the chief executive officers of the seven largest US tobacco manufacturers testified, under oath, that they believed cigarettes were neither addictive nor harmful. I've no stomach for that sort of thing.

"I got sick of my job, Robert, and then I got sick with a vengeance. My lungs are trashed, and I barely survived that surgery. I still find it hard to believe that my cancer wasn't actually caused by smoking."

"You're being very frank," said Robert.

"I have to face the facts. The big question for me now is, *what have I done for others and what have I learned?*"

"I think I understand, Joe," said Robert.

"You do, Robert. You understand me, and smoking as a personal issue. But I don't think that you understand about nicotine as big business. Global, international business."

"You're right, Joe," Robert said. "That's not my field."

"Let me put it this way for you, Robert. The Canadian public spends perhaps $8 billion dollars on tobacco every year," Joe said, "and there are ten times as many smokers in the United States. Then there's the rest of the world. Money talks, and big money only needs to whisper in order to get things done. Tobacco Incorporated kills, but it survives."

Robert was at a loss for words. On an impulse, he reached for the envelope on his desk and handed it to Joe, who opened it and stared fixedly at the memos. His expression betrayed no reaction.

"I found that under your chair, Joe," Robert said.

"Nobody else has seen it or knows about it. It was with me when the office was broken into, and has stayed with me or in my safety deposit box ever since."

There was a pause in their exchange as Joe stared fixedly at the paper in his hand.

"But you must know people in tobacco control who would be interested in this?" Joe asked, without looking up.

"Sure. Bill Brown* is a good friend of mine who's trying to gather exactly that kind of evidence about the internal policies of tobacco companies."

"Who is he, a lawyer?"

"No, he's a university professor who simply believes in justice and doing his part to promote it."

"Why didn't you give this to him?" Joe asked.

"I didn't come by it honestly, Joe. Anything discussed in this room is strictly confidential, and that has to include papers you might accidentally leave behind."

"I see," said Joe. He pocketed the memo, then reached out and grasped Robert's hand, shaking it firmly. "Thanks for taking care of it for me."

Joe then cut short the session and any further discussion of the memos by smoothly changing the subject. The next session would be their last, he said. Robin and he were planning an extended holiday beginning in June. They were going to China first, on to India to visit some charity that Robin supported, and then would go exploring. He wanted to get right away from his usual life.

After arranging to meet again in another three weeks, Joe collected his helmet and jacket and disappeared.

Robert heard the motorcycle start up, then quickly recede into the city sounds. He felt drained, and left to go for a long walk. He would wonder if he had done the right thing.

*fictitious name

* * * * *

Robert's note for the day:

Joe is not smoking, into the maintenance stage now.

Today's was an unusual session. I accidentally provoked him into justifying his past career by commenting that he used to be very good at what he did, in other words selling cigarettes. He had quite a strong reaction. Unfortunately I'm not sure how much we accomplished today. Something's up, but I'm not sure what.

Next week: for our last session we must talk about relapse.

15

Holding The Line

The world is a very fine place and worth the fighting for and I hate very much to leave it.

— Hemingway

JUST AS ROBERT was about to settle down to some writing, the phone rang. A familiar voice returned his greeting.

"Doctor Borenot, I presume?" It was his friend Professor Bill Brown, from the university. "Robert, the most extraordinary thing has happened and I need your advice. I've just received several boxes of internal documents from a major tobacco company."

"What?"

"A package arrived on my doorstep yesterday, from an anonymous source. I've only had a chance to glance at some of them, but I can say that they are extremely incriminating."

"Are you pulling my leg?"

"Not at all."

Eventually the documents would be donated to the university library. The tobacco company from which the documents apparently originated would seek an injunction to prevent their circulation, but it would be rejected by the courts.

The documents would support litigation against the tobacco industry, and spur the American president to have the Food and Drug Administration (FDA) assume jurisdiction over tobacco.

* * * * *

May 5th

ROBERT USHERED ROBIN AND JOE into his office for the final session. He hung up their jackets and offered them fresh coffee. Two large bouquets of fresh flowers blossomed in tall vases on either side of their chairs.

They had arranged to dine out together afterwards.

"Stopping smoking is cause for celebration," Robert declared, when Joe commented on the decorations. Besides

Joe's success at not smoking, Robert was also privately celebrating the news of the leaked documents. He was eager to ask Joe about them.

"Before we get started, Joe, let me clear my mind of something. A friend of mine has recently received a bit of a windfall, confidential documents from an anonymous source in a major tobacco company. You wouldn't happen to know anything about them, by any chance?"

"Really?" Joe asked. "I imagine that some of that stuff could be quite embarrassing. Well, well. Whoever leaked it, and whoever touches it, for that matter, could be sued for silence from here to eternity and back."

"You... don't know anything about it then?" Robert hesitantly asked.

"I'd rather not." Did Joe wink ever so slightly as he spoke? "Say, I'd rather talk about dealing with cravings to smoke, and staying smoke-free."

Robert smiled to himself, knowing that indeed it must have been Joe who'd blown the whistle on the tobacco industry's antics.

Together they reviewed Joe's record. He hadn't smoked at all until a few days after their last meeting, when he'd had a terrible day and a couple of drinks at an office party held in his honor.

"I didn't really want to be there," Joe explained. "I'm putting my tobacco past behind me, and under the circumstances a smoky office party wasn't exactly ideal. After a few toasts to this and that I began to feel I had to have a cigarette, in the worst way."

"Alcohol can do that. What happened then?"

"I picked a cigarette from the pack the waiter always carries on his tray, and started smoking. It felt both good and bad. Still very familiar, you know."

"Of course, Joe. It had only been a few weeks since you stopped. You've gotten out of the ruts in the road, but they're still there and just as deep. One of the problems ex-smokers often encounter is over-confidence. Before they've really established their non-smoking selves, they go back into situations where the urge to smoke is bound to be strong."

"Yeah, you'd warned me about that. It gets a bit worse."

Robin interrupted and put her hand on Joe's arm.

"Honey, it's not a bad thing at all," she said. "Slips can happen. Nobody's perfect. Did you really expect to never smoke another, after thirty years of steady smoking?"

Joe smiled. He looked relaxed, and healthier than Robert had ever seem him.

"After leaving that party I asked the taxi to stop so I could buy a pack," he said. "I have no idea why I did that. And I smoked another right away."

"Tricky little monkey, isn't he?" Robert said. They all had a chuckle at the reference to the nicotine-monkey.

"I learned a big lesson that night. When I finally got home I smelt like a smoked herring, of course, and when she kissed me Robin knew right away I'd been smoking."

"Yuuuk!" Robin said. "Ever lick an ashtray?"

"But she was great about it, and reminded me about the rules of relapse. I took that pack and shredded it into the toilet before flushing it away. I learned what to avoid, and how to handle it anyway."

"Good for you, Joe. You did really well. Remember, the worst times for cravings are periods of high stress, and when you're feeling overconfident and expose yourself to temptation. Occasionally somebody will tell me about how they quit while keeping a full pack in their pocket, always available. I don't recommend it at all, because that makes it just too easy to smoke again. And it figures that you didn't buy that first cigarette you smoked, at the party. Most people 'slip' with smokes they bum from somebody else, if you'll excuse the expression. Never smoke a cigarette you didn't buy for yourself.

"And one more thing. I think it's great how you support each other. Other people are the most important resource you have, besides your own inner fire."

"But I didn't support Robin at all," said Joe. "It was she who helped me."

"Isn't trusting in other people a sort of gift to them, though? It gives them the opportunity to try and help. We all want to feel useful and needed, and there's no greater gift than gratitude. So you supported Robin, too. Consider how different both of you would feel now if you had hidden your smoking for awhile, then resumed as before."

Joe readily agreed.

"What's more, Joe, I've learned a great deal about tobacco and smoking from you. So thank you. And by the way, are there any particular times when you experience urges to smoke? How do you deal with them? I might be able to help someone else learn from your experience."

Joe seemed pleasantly surprised at the compliment, and the opportunity.

"Oh, I still get the urge fairly often. But I use physical activity a lot. I'll go for a quick walk outside if I can, or just go and climb a few flights of stairs. I get so out of breath that it reminds me that's how I'd probably always feel, if I kept smoking into my old age. But you know what? It's getting easier to do a few flights. And I don't have to use my asthma puffer as often."

"That's great. Shall we test your lungs, and know your numbers* as the experts suggest? Robert didn't wait for an answer but brought out the spirometer again. "Do your best!" he urged, as Joe exhaled into the mouthpiece.

* "Test Your Lungs / Know Your Numbers" is the motto of the National Lung Health Education Program.

"Hmmm. Not bad. There's been some improvement already," Robert observed, comparing the tracing with Joe's previous attempt. "You'll need to keep an eye on that, of course, but stopping smoking is simply the best thing you could possibly have done for your lungs."

"And what a relief it is. But you know, I've heard so many stories about people smoking again years after having quit. How does that happen? What can I do to prevent it?"

"Even after five years, Joe, perhaps a quarter of ex-smokers aren't completely confident about their ability to resist the temptation to smoke again, in difficult circumstances. Keep your guard up, don't kid yourself that you can ever smoke 'just one,' and if you do start, stop again right away."

"I hope I'll be able to do that."

"Call me if you ever need any help, Joe. Remember that people quit and start again several times before they get free. About three quarters of smokers who quit will be at it again within twelve months. But the more you try, the more chance you have of succeeding. So stopping smoking is a process that may take a couple of years at least. Don't be discouraged by persistent urges to smoke. Just keep at it. But I'm repeating myself. Tell me, are there any other techniques you use to deal with cravings?"

Robin was the first to speak. "For the very worst times, Joe goes for a motorcycle ride. There's some canyon roads not far from our home, and he loves to smooth out the curves there, as he puts it."

"Really? That's great. I've known motorcyclists who could somehow roll, light, and smoke a cigarette with one hand at sixty miles an hour, but that would be impossible on a demanding road. Joe, I've got an idea."

"Oh, no!" Joe quipped. "Not another stress demonstration! You'd better tell me what you have in mind."

"I just had an idea for a hypnotic suggestion that might help you in the long run. Would you like to go for a ride on the smoke-cycle right now?"

"Only if I'm driving," Joe said, somewhat hesitantly. With Robert's hypnosis, Joe was sometimes unsure exactly what he was getting himself into.

"Of course," Robert said.

"I'd like to see how that works," said Robin. When she'd consulted Robert years before, he hadn't been using any hypnosis. So Joe obliged.

He settled back in his chair, and Robert began to speak softly, pausing between sentences. "Stretch out and close your eyes, Joe, and just follow your breath in and out... Find the relaxation in your body.... Let it happen.... Slow breath in.... Slow breath out...." He continued on in that vein for a few minutes, inducing a deep hypnotic trance as he had during several of their previous sessions.

Robin watched, fascinated. Joe appeared to be resting peacefully, holding the "handlebars" of his chair.

"Imagine that you decide to go for a ride in the mountains on your motorcycle. It's a beautiful day and you laugh with joy as you roll up the winding route to a high pass. You notice something strange about the road. The white center-line is actually a series of cigarettes painted on the road.

"Then suddenly you pass the summit, the way steepens, and you find yourself racing just slightly out of control down the other side."

Joe sat forward and balanced on the edge of his chair.

"You want to stop, but can't. It's all you can do to stay on the twisty and treacherously narrow ribbon of asphalt. You feel the rush of the speed, the hurricane wind flowing around you. The center line becomes a solid stream of white. Look out for that corner ahead!"

Joe's breathing became more rapid and his eyelids and arms were twitching with the visualization.

"You quickly grab the brakes but there's something wrong. They don't work very well. Suddenly you have to let go of them and steer through the next corner. That was close! And you're still fairly falling down the mountain at a tremendous speed, with more to come.

"Now, do you give up? Do you decide that you'll never be able to stop? Or use those brakes at every opportunity?

"Don't stop stopping, Joe. Get the feel of the process. You downshift before sweeping round some tricky curves. Watch out for slippery patches! You rein in your ride sharply wherever there's enough traction. Finally, you come to a halt at the side of the road. There's a perfect place to rest.

"You get off the habit and know you've finally stopped for good. You immediately check the brakes on the machine. Wisps of smoke smelling of burnt tar curl upwards from them before dissipating in the light breeze. It's a good thing you kept stopping at every opportunity, Joe.

"It's a beautiful day in the mountains. You take off your helmet and breathe the clean, fresh air. There's no traffic and you can hear birds singing in the woods. Now you walk to the centerline of the road. Sure enough, it's a series of painted-on cigarettes, advertisements for different brands.

"You're glad to be alive. After your brush with death, there's a special quality to each moment. Colors seem sharper, every breath more fulfilling, and each moment more glorious. You notice the unpainted asphalt between the cigarettes, and the space, the emptiness, now seems much more important than the lure of the smokes."

Joe was now resting peacefully.

"Your gaze moves up and away from the road, and you see the exceptional beauty of the place. When you turn to get back on your bike you notice that the centerline is just simple lines once again. The brakes on your machine work fine now, and you're in perfect control.

"At the count of five you'll park your bike and wake up, and remember everything that happened. One, two, three, four... five. Welcome back, Joe."

Joe opened his eyes with a grin.

"How does that work?" Robin asked.

"It's a technique that occasionally works," Robert said, "but it isn't any better than any other approach. It's just something that helps some people. You really don't need any fancy approach to quitting, or to staying smoke-free. Preparation and persistence always pay off. You've got to press on, and burn the bridges behind you."

"Thanks, Robert," said Joe.

"And thank you from me," said Robin. "Speaking of pressing on, didn't we have a reservation somewhere?"

It was indeed time to go. They walked over to a small restaurant not far from Robert's office. The owner met them at the door with a smile. "Good evening madam," he said. "and gentlemen. Will that be non-smoking, or smoke-free?"

"That's Carlo's way of letting you know he won't permit smoking here," Robert explained as they took their places. They ordered their meals and enjoyed some appetizers while discussing the state of the world and various solutions. Environmental disasters and neglect, poverty, wars, ill-health. Naturally enough, the conversation kept returning to how people can best quit smoking.

"You know what else I found really helped?" Robin said. "I took the money I saved from not smoking and sent it off to a charity. I know it isn't much, about two grand a year, but every little bit makes a difference."

Robert was quite taken by this idea. He knew that for older smokers, providing an example to children and grandchildren could be a tremendous motivation to quit. Sometimes people would be more willing to help others than themselves. He urged Robin to tell him more.

She pulled something from her purse and handed it to Robert: a newsletter.

"Child Haven is a wonderful organization that operates orphanages in poor countries," she said. "This extraordinary couple adopted *nineteen* children from around the world after having two of their own. Can you imagine that?"

Having chosen to have no children of his own, Robert found the thought of raising *twenty-one* a bit daunting.

"But wait, that's not all. Once those kids had grown up, Bonnie and Fred Cappuccino set up homes for *four hundred* orphans in India and Nepal. Besides shelter and food they get an education and a loving family. We're going to visit the places on our trip."

She offered to send Robert some more information and he eagerly accepted. The name and the story was familiar, from somewhere. He thought he'd seen the couple years before on the "Man Alive" television program.

"How wonderful," said Robert. "That goes to show what faith and focus can do. Every little action adds up, doesn't it? Raindrops make a river."

Neither Robin nor Joe answered, so Robert continued: "I have a fantasy that every smoker in North America could use one less cigarette daily, for one year, and donate all the money saved to the charity of their choice."

"A drop in the bucket," said Joe emphatically.

"One point eight billion dollars?" Robert asked. "That's quite a drop, no matter how big the bucket."

"But it would cost more to collect the money than it would be worth," Joe objected.

"Not necessarily," said Robert. "There could simply be a tax on cigarette manufacture. The cost would be passed on to consumers, who'd smoke less."

"I doubt it," Joe responded. "Nicotine demands consistency. People would just spend more to smoke."

Robin interrupted to point out that higher prices for cigarettes do reduce consumption, especially among young people. In 1994 when tobacco taxes were reduced in some Canadian provinces but not in others, smoking by adolescents increased where it had become cheaper. "We have to make cigarettes less appealing to young non-smokers," she insisted. "Isn't raising tobacco taxes a good approach?"

"Now wait a minute, kids," said Joe. "Aren't you being slightly naive? Robert, you do remember saying that you have no right to pass judgement on anybody else's life, or something like that?"

Robert nodded, with a slightly sheepish grin.

"Then you can't lay a guilt trip on people by dangling the cost of their choice in front of their faces, whether you measure it in money or the state of their health. They smoke, and choose not to tackle their addiction, for their own good reasons. And Robin, my dear, you'd like to mobilize the world for your particular cause but there are many others. You'd like to raise taxes to coerce people not to smoke. But just look at me."

Joe paused to sip from his water glass because he was a performer at heart, and wanted to create some suspense.

"I'm Joe K. Hamel. I know tobacco. I know the industry. I know nicotine, personally and professionally. I know smoking. And I assure you that people will smoke when they want to. Nicotine transforms life. Worries don't matter, for a few minutes. Time even waits for you, while you smoke. It's a sacred herb."

Robin and Robert listened to Joe's speech, motionless.

"Yes," Joe continued. "Tobacco has a unique appeal. I know. I know smoking. Strong. Independent. Proud. Cool. I know that feeling, which we exploited so effectively. I know the smoke, the rush, the relaxation."

Joe paused again, looked them in the eyes, and finally made his point.

"It's a lie. I also know the daily grind of smoking, when it seems like a mindless obligation. I also know the loss of any good feeling, as the nicotine lets you down. I've been through the fire. And you know, there still isn't a day that I don't think about smoking."

Joe smiled and leaned back in his chair.

"And I'm so satisfied not to need nicotine anymore. I'm over the hump. I know smoking, and I can do without the hassle, the cost, the cough, the cancers, the heart disease, and so on. The whole damn price of smoking. I know smoking, and I've come to hate it."

Robin applauded. "Bravo, Joe." Robert said.

"Besides," Joe added, "I can always use Ecitonin."

"Use what?" Robin and Joe asked in unison.

"Fantastic drug. This is top-secret, so you mustn't tell anyone. I've been doing some consulting on a new product that may hit the market within the next year."

"Joe! You didn't tell me about this!" said Robin, her face visibly flushed and her eyes seeming to light up the table.

"It's simple to administer," Joe continued, "and the mild relaxation effect is almost immediate. I've tried it myself, and I believe the marketing people when they say that we'll sell billions of dollars worth every year."

"Joe!" said Robin. "You what?!"

"There are some minor drawbacks to the product," Joe admitted, ignoring his wife's outrage. "One of the most worrisome is that the delivery system seems to produce a variety of diseases."

"Surely it won't ever be licensed," argued Robert.

"Oh yes it will. In fact it's already got government approval, and they expect big taxes from it, much like alcohol. I must admit the side effects cause me some concern. For example, it seems that every second user will die from a disease caused by the delivery system, and that Ecitonin itself is highly addictive."

Robert started laughing, and Robin's bewilderment was now replaced with an "I'll-get-you-later" grin.

"I'm talking about tobacco smoking, of course," Joe continued. "*Ecitonin* is *nicotine* with the letters rearranged. If I tried to introduce a product like that today, I'd be considered a lunatic or a psychopath. But tobacco is just, well, good old tobacco. Everybody is habituated to it."

Their supper arrived just then. Robert and Robin were speechless, anyway. They all tucked into an excellent meal. Robert suddenly put down his knife and fork.

"You know, Joe," he said. "I've never really thought about it that way. Not really ever thought about it."

* * * * *

The clinical note:

Joe is doing well, on Day 65. I hope he lives smoke-free and contented for many years to come. He's taught me a lot.

16

Ashes, Dust, and Eternity

Despite man's tendency to live on low and degrading planes, something reminds him that he is not made for that. As he trails in the dust, something reminds him that he is made for the stars. As he makes folly his bedfellow, a nagging inner voice tells him he is born for eternity.
> *— Martin Luther King, Jr.*

May 31st

(World No-Tobacco Day)

The occasional postcard in the following months kept Robert informed of Joe and Robin's progress. Sandy beaches, stunning mountains, and according to the hastily-scribbled notes, still no smoking.

Robert had certainly never had such an unusual client as Joe, one with so much to win or lose playing tobacco. He was a high-stakes gambler who'd blown the whistle on the crooked dealers. Actually Robert still wasn't sure, but it must have been Joe that delivered those documents to Bill Brown.

Once the leaked papers were analyzed and catalogued they pointed beyond any reasonable doubt to a most distressing conclusion; certain sectors of the tobacco industry had long known that their product was addictive and harmful, and had deceived the American government and people by concealing that knowledge.

The American Medical Association (AMA) published an extensive analysis of the documents in one of its monthly journals, concluding with the following statement:

"In summary, the evidence is unequivocal. The U.S. public has been duped by the tobacco industry. No right-thinking individual can ignore the evidence. We should all be outraged, and we should force the removal of this scourge from our nation and by so doing set an example for the world. We recognize the serious consequences of this ambition, but the health of our nation is more important than the profits of any single industry. On behalf of the physicians of this country and the people they serve, the American Medical Association pledges its best efforts to the eradication of tobacco-related disease. We solicit the support of the public and our government in this endeavor. It is a worthy cause."

Robert sat in his office thinking about his work. Not much had really changed, since the AMA had made their statement. Tobacco advertising of one form or another was still permitted, much of it obviously aimed at children.

Sometimes Robert doubted that he was making much difference by helping individual smokers. "Treating the smoke but not the fire," as he'd say. Perhaps the solution lies in not feeding the flames. Tobacco is an addictive substance, the major reversible cause of disease and death in the developed world, and it victimizes the unsuspecting. But it's advertised and sold like an expensive chocolate bar.

Who exactly is responsible for the tobacco epidemic? Governments treat cigarette taxes as general revenue, and politicians accept perfectly legal contributions of tobacco money. Doctors don't always ask patients about smoking, or press political leaders to control tobacco. Investors take the money and run, perhaps unknowingly assuming part of the blame through their pension plans or mutual funds. Smokers themselves are only part of the picture.

Perhaps there's no use spitting into the wind, Robert thought. Things may never change. From the jumble on his desk he picked out the Child Haven International newsletter that Robin had given him. A quote on the front page caught his eye: "'*Let me light my lamp,' said the star, 'and never ask whether it will dispel the darkness.*'"

Just then the phone rang. It was a courier with a special delivery parcel. Robert descended to collect it.

The small package bore a Hazardous Materials sticker. According to the waybill it had been sent from a Hong Kong law office. Robert signed for the shipment and returned to his desk, much intrigued. He began to rip off the wrapping, but suddenly stopped.

Hazardous materials? Robert thought he detected a faint aroma of something volatile in the package. It couldn't be a bomb, he thought, and laughed out loud. Some kind of joke, perhaps? A pound of tobacco?

He opened his prize to discover a couple of letters and another small package about the size of two matchboxes that was wrapped in tissue paper.

Dear Robert,

We're alive and well. Joe had a complete check-up in Singapore, and there's no sign of any recurrence of his cancer. He hasn't smoked at all in going on four months now. We think of you often, and with very warm wishes for your health and happiness.

We first flew to Thailand, where after getting used to the heat we spent a few days at a Buddhist monastery learning to meditate. My choice. Joe wasn't sure what to make of it but he continues to sit in silent relaxation for ten minutes daily. I believe it helps him to relax, and stay smoke-free.

Joe hasn't gained any more weight despite his new-found taste buds (Thai cooking is exceptional!). I must say that all his appetites have increased since he quit smoking, and we get plenty of exercise.

It was a short hop by plane to India where we visited each of the three Child Haven homes. The little children were so inspired! Each of them had been snatched back from a miserable fate and an early death through the stubborn perseverance and compassion of Bonnie and Fred and their supporters. (I hope you've had a chance to look at their newsletter.)

From India we traveled by road to Nepal, through a particularly poverty-stricken region of India. Even a small bit of help would make a huge difference for these people, who still fetch their water from polluted streams and live in deplorable conditions.

Joe's old colleagues wouldn't have believed their eyes if they had seen him giving classes on how to stop smoking, in a dusty Indian village. Lots of pantomime, lots of laughter and joy.

In Nepal we hiked for a month around the Annapurna range of mountains, crossing a high pass at 17,000 feet above sea-level. Joe had to use bottled oxygen through the pass and of course he wasn't able to carry his own pack. But one year ago he couldn't have hiked to such an extraordinarily beautiful place, even with assistance.

After Nepal we flew to Tibet and then made our way overland into China. Joe has become very interested in tobacco again, but from a different perspective: he wanted to attend the 11th World Congress on Tobacco and Health. The conference in Beijing was quite fascinating with presentations on every aspect of smoking and tobacco control.

Joe is planning to start a foundation to help educate people in developing countries about the harmful effects of tobacco. He's much happier, healthier, and contented now than I believe I've ever known him to be.

After China we joined up in Singapore with some old friends who have a sailing yacht, and plan on making our way home via the South Pacific Islands. For the moment we're enjoying this brief lull before the storm that's sure to break when Joe gets busy with his non-smoking activities. He has truly undergone a remarkable transformation.

Thank-you once again, Robert.

Robin

p.s. Good luck with your book.

The second letter was from Joe.

Dear Robert,

I hope you're keeping well. I'm proud and delighted to report that I've been smoke-free since we last met; I can breathe easier, taste food again, and almost keep up with Robin. I swear it feels better not to smoke, today, right now, than it ever did to smoke, and I can't imagine ever taking up the habit again.

Sorry I didn't write or phone sooner. Although we're supposedly on holiday, there doesn't seem to be enough time to do everything we want to and more to the point, I'm at a loss to describe how my life has changed since we last met.

Robin mentioned that we spent a few days at a monastery learning to meditate, which reminded me a bit of the start of your hypnosis sessions: relaxation and inward focus.

After that we visited the Child Haven homes, where Robin spent our money just as she'd promised. I love it.

I had an extraordinary experience outside one small Indian village where I'd been giving lessons about smoking —but that's another story. I was able to slip away for a quiet walk and discovered a huge ant-hill with columns of ants coming and going like suburban commuters.

For some reason I sat down to watch their activity, and found myself trying to imagine what the ant-hill would be like if they smoked like we do. There would have to be better ventilation or everybody would die. And some sort of hospital area with doctor and nurse ants, and so on. Considerable labor would go into caring for the sick and dying, and some into growing and processing tobacco.

I thought how odd we humans are. We've explored and exploited our world to the point that we can fly across oceans, put men on the moon, and split the atom, but we kill ourselves at an extraordinary rate with tobacco.

A speaker at the Beijing conference explained a few of the connections between tobacco and poverty. Many resources are diverted to care for those harmed by smoking. Apparently the global expenses of tobacco-related death, disability, and medical treatment are at least $200 billion more than the economic benefits of tobacco.

So that's the ant-hill story. We live in a paradise, Robert, but waste it. What's a fellow to do? Robin dragged me around the Child Haven homes is India and Nepal, where I saw the hope for the future in the children. They would still be desperate and destitute, if they hadn't gotten a second chance. I think they'll grow up with a deep appreciation for life, and perhaps help us out of this mess we're in.

I've been given a second chance, too, and I'm making some plans to make a difference. The next time somebody asks me what I've learned and what I've done for others, I intend to have satisfactory answers.

Robin and I will be establishing some kind of foundation to educate people about smoking. I don't want to become a sanctimonious ex-smoker; I just want to make sure that people know the facts.

There are times when I feel quite strong cravings to smoke again, usually when I'm worrying about something. I find that if I just do nothing, other than practicing some deep breathing, the urge passes.

Whether it's my body recovering or the different perspective I now have on life, I don't know, but I seem to have more energy and stamina these days.

Thanks again for all your help.

Your (ex-smoker) friend,

Joe

Robert picked up the smaller package and found it quite heavy for its size. Unwrapping the tissue paper packaging he found... Joe's lighter.

He felt the heft of the solid gold, and noticed for the first time the initials 'R.B.' set in precious stones on the top. There was a fresh-looking inscription on the back, also:

FOR ROBERT, WITH THANKS

FOR BURNING BRIDGES

Flicking it open with one hand, he spun the striker-wheel.

Sparks ignited the waiting wick.

The flame burned hot, and clean.

* * * * *

The End

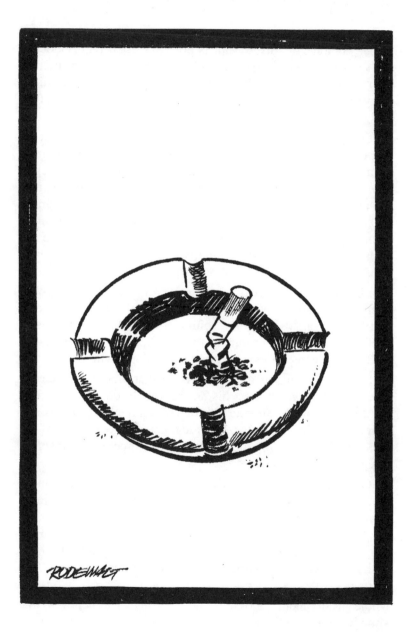

ABOUT THE AUTHOR

Dr. Simon Timothy Bryant is not your usual family doctor. He's a man with a simple but ambitious mission: to ensure that everybody knows the whole truth about smoking and quitting. Why? Because he wants to empower people to help themselves and others enjoy healthier, happier, and longer lives.

From an early age, Simon explored the world and some of its possibilities. He came from England at the age of 3 and grew up in French-speaking Quebec, but his adventuring really began when he bicycled alone for 3,000 miles across the continent at the age of 13. In his adolescence he worked as a welder and a machinist and raced motorcycles. Seeking greater fulfillment he spent a couple of years learning to grow a garden and build log houses, while assisting the mentally ill at an experimental "half-way" house; tough work, but rewarding.

Simon next spent two years as a group leader for a youth exchange program, living in remote rural villages in Indonesia and Sri Lanka. After briefly volunteering at Mother Theresa's shelter in Calcutta, he returned to Canada to obtain a Bachelor of Science degree in Psychology and Biology, with distinction.

Simon then turned to a profession that would provide his greatest challenge and test his desire to help others: medicine. By the time Dr. Bryant had completed his medical studies and training as a family doctor, he'd developed a keen sense of the preventable tragedy of smoking and felt compelled to do something about it.

Over the next few years Dr. Bryant focused his attention on that issue, reviewing the literature and attending international conferences. He served as a Clinical Lecturer at the University of Calgary, and as a director of Physicians for A Smoke-Free Canada. He learned that people appreciate being told the facts with compassion and perhaps a touch of humor.

This book is part of Dr. Bryant's mission to offer people the whole truth about smoking and quitting, He believes that knowledge can provide the power and inspiration to heal oneself and others.

(Bonnie and Fred Cappuccino)

With the help of many volunteers, support groups, and donors, Child Haven now operates three homes for destitute orphans in India and one in Nepal. Child Haven was founded in 1985 and is now registered as a charitable, non-sectarian organization in the United States, Canada, India, and Nepal.

Children from birth to six years of age are referred to us by local social welfare agencies. Child Haven homes provide full care and support through high school and then arrange further vocational training. Our goal is to help each child develop into a self-sufficient adult.

In our homes boys and girls are treated equally without regard to race, caste, color, religion or culture. Living is simple and meals are vegetarian. We try not to westernize the children and make a conscious attempt to raise them according to the highest ideals of their own cultures and religions, whether Hindu, Muslim, Jain, Christian, Buddhist, secular or other.

Our international network includes support groups, donors, volunteers and friends around the world. They work together in their own ways to raise public awareness and bring attention to the plight of destitute women and children in India and Nepal. Since 1985 approximately 200 volunteers have paid their own way to help out at the homes themselves, in various capacities. The existence of Child Haven depends on the generosity and enthusiasm of these individuals and support groups, and we thank them.

Our Programs for Women

Child Haven is committed to improving the condition of women through direct employment, education, legal aid, and training opportunities. We're delighted with the local enthusiasm for our Women's Tailoring Unit in India. Our literacy programs and typing programs are popular with local women and youths.

Child Haven has created employment for over 100 women in India and Nepal, as of 1995. Disadvantaged women are presently receiving training in tailoring, weaving, and computer science. Over 50 women in various parts of India have been trained in the operation and maintenance of Soya Cows, the efficient machines which transform soya beans into nutritious soya milk.

The Soya Cow Project

A Soya Cow machine makes 3 gallons of nutritious soya milk from 3.7 pounds of raw soybeans, in 30 minutes. This simple technology produces a palatable, high protein, cereal or almond flavored milk without cholesterol.

Child Haven promotes this technology and uses the machines in their homes. Soya milk is a low cost, high protein product which is cheaper to produce than cow's milk. Ten times as much soya milk can be produced from a piece of land, at half the cost of cow's milk.

At Child Haven schools and homes, soya milk made on the premises is safe from contamination by dilution with unsafe water. It's also free from tuberculosis or other diseases from infected cows.

Your Contribution

Your donation goes where it's needed most, to the homes for destitute children, because Child Haven keeps administrative costs to a bare minimum. Indian and Nepalese staff in the homes are paid according to local wage scales. Volunteers pay their own airfare and receive no salary. A minimal salary is shared between the two directors, Bonnie and Fred Cappuccino, and a bookkeeper. Support Group members and volunteers provide communication, administration, publication and technical assistance at no charge to Child Haven.

In 1993, a Child Haven home in India provided care for 96 children and cost (in U.S. dollars):

$6,815 per year salaries paid to 23 Indian staff at local rates.

$289 rent per month

$648 food per month

$294 school uniforms and tuition annually.

$2267 utilities and cooking fuel annually.

$912 medical annually.

Please consider using the coupon on the facing page now.

Child Haven International
Accueil International Pour L'Enfance
RR#1, Maxville, ON, K0C 1T0, Canada

Phone 613–527–2829, FAX 613–527–1118

Child Haven is a registered non-profit charitable organization in Canada, USA, India and Nepal.

Registered charitable numbers:
Canada 0707034–01 USA 22-2637689
India Vide Lt. No. 11/1A+80G/20/90–91

I would like my contribution to be used:

☐ Wherever it is needed most

☐ 24-hour care of destitute children in Child Haven homes

☐ Work with women (Soyamilk and technical training)

☐ Medical care

☐ Refugees (abroad or in Canada)

1. I would like to contribute $ _____ (enclosed). Cheques may be made out to Child Haven.

2. I would like to sponsor Child Haven's program in India and Nepal at $14 per month. (Please check method of payment):

annually	$168	☐
semi-annually	$84	☐
quarterly	$42	☐
monthly	$14	☐

Post-dated cheques are accepted.

☐ I would like information about doing volunteer work in India. (Volunteers pay their own travel, currently about $1400, live at children's homes on vegetarian meals, and receive no salary. Three months minimum commitment.)

Name _____

Address _____

City _____Province/State _____

Zip/Postal Code _____Phone _____

USA friends can save "out of country" postage by mailing to Child Haven, Box 5099, Massena, NY 13662-5099

Recommended Books

These books are listed as a service to readers, because I think they would be particularly useful to smokers and/or health care providers. Please be sure to mention where you learned of them, when ordering.

Changing For Good: the revolutionary program that explains the six stages of change and teaches you how to free yourself from bad habits.
James O. Prochaska, Ph.D., John C. Norcross, Ph.D., and Carlo C. DiClemente, Ph.D.
Dr. Prochaska and his colleagues are leaders in describing the psychology of human behavior-change, and present their important theory with enthusiasm and clarity. Whatever lifestyle change a person makes, they go through the same six stages: precontemplation, contemplation, preparation, action, maintenance, and termination. Of interest to health-care providers and people who want to understand the process of change.
ISBN 0-688-11263-3. William Morrow and Company, 1994
Hardcover, 304 pages, bibliography, index. $34.95 Canada
(paperback also available)

How Women Can (Finally) Quit Smoking
Robert C. Klesges and Margaret DeBon
My favorite recommendation for women who smoke. Provides practical solutions to the unique problems that women face when trying to stop smoking, or finding the motivation to do so.
ISBN 0-89793-147-5. Hunter House, 1994.
Paperback, 180 pages, references, index.
$8.95 U.S., $12.95 Canada
1-800-266-5982

Motivational Interviewing: preparing people to change addictive behavior
William R. Miller and Stephan Rollnick
If you counsel people with addictions, you must read this book.
ISBN 0-89862-566-1. Guilford Press, 1991.
Paperback, 348 pages, references, index. $29.95 Canada

If Only I Could Quit: recovering from nicotine addiction
Karen Casey
Learn from others' experience. The accounts of 23 everyday ex-smokers, many incorporating a '12-step' approach to smoke-free living. Includes 90 daily 'meditations' for recent ex-smokers.
ISBN 0-89486-438-6. Hazelden Foundation, 1987.
Paperback, 300 pages, index.
1-800-328-9000 (U.S. only) / (612) 257-4010 (outside U.S.)

The Last Puff:
Ex-smokers share the secrets of their success
John W. Farquhar, M.D., and Gene A. Spiller, Ph.D.
Thirty former smokers, mostly quite well-educated, share how they managed to quit. Like "If Only I Could Quit," this book is not a step-by-step approach to quitting, but is a compelling collection of true stories.
ISBN 0-393-30803-0. W.W. Norton, 1990
Paperback, 252 pages. $9.95 USA, $12.99 Canada

Stop Smoking Without putting On Weight
Penny Ross
Penny Ross , an ex-smoker and nutritionist, understands weight problems and nicotine addiction from both a personal and a professional perspective. She provides effective techniques for handling the emotional aspects of both weight control and stopping smoking.
ISBN 0-7225-3015-3. Thorsons, 1992
Paperback, 173 pages, indexed. $5.99 USA, $7.99 Canadian

How To Quit Smoking Without Gaining Weight
Martin Katahn
A calorie-counting approach to weight control, with some
basic information about quitting smoking. Includes recipes,
appendices on strength training, relaxation training, and a 48-
page fine-print listing of fat and carbohydrate content of thou-
sands of foods.
ISBN 0-393-03714-2
Hardcover, 223 pages, 5.25" x 7.25", index.
$12.95 USA, $16.99 Canada (Paperback now available)

SmokeScreen: a guide to the personal risks and global
effects of the cigarette habit
Barry J Ford
An easy-to-read reference book, beautifully illustrated with
numerous color photos, diagrams, and old tobacco advertise-
ments. Chapter summaries and extensive references make this
a very practical tool. A must for all health care professionals,
libraries, and those who simply want the facts. Well worth
ordering and waiting for. Not to be confused with
"Smokescreen: the truth behind the tobacco industry cover-
up" by Philip J. Hilts.
ISBN 0-646-10564-7 (paperback)
ISBN 0-646-14148-1 (hardcover), Halcyon, 1994.
Paperback, 242 pages, chapter summaries, references, index.
Halycon Press, PO Box 21, North Perth
WA 6006, Australia
fax 61-9-227-1295
tel. 61-9-328-4873

The No-Nag, No-Guilt, Do-It-Your-Own-Way Guide To Quitting Smoking
Tom Ferguson, MD
My personal favorite. It not only covers the essentials of getting ready to quit and becoming a permanent non-smoker, but also includes information on health strategies, nutrition and vitamins, and much more.Written in 1987, it remains an extremely helpful book, and excellent value.
ISBN 0-345-35578-4. Ballantine Books, 1989.
Paperback, 330 pages, bibliography, index.
$5.99 US, $6.99 Canada   1-800-433-3803 / (503) 520-5285

The Stop Smoking Workbook: your guide to healthy quitting.
Anita Maximin, Psy.D., & Lori Stevic-Rust, Ph.D.
This is a very up-to-date workbook which takes the reader step-by-step through the stages of becoming smoke-free. For the smoker who wants to change, this is an excellent resource.
ISBN 1-57224-037-7. New Harbinger Publications, Inc., 1996
Softcover workbook.
U.S. $17.95 Canadian $25.95
New Harbinger Publications, Inc.,
5674 Shattuck Avenue
Oakland, CA 94609

Selected Bibliography

Bartecchi C, Mackenzie T, Schrier R. The Global Tobacco Epidemic. *Scientific American*, May 1995.

Benowitz NL. Cigarette smoking and nicotine addiction. *Medical Clinics of North America*, Vol. 76(2), 1992.

Baer JS, Marlatt GA. Maintenance of smoking cessation. *Clinics in Chest Medicine*, Vol. 12(4), 1991.

Chapman S, Wong W, Smith W. Self-Exempting Beliefs About Smoking and Health: Differences Between Smokers and Ex-smokers. *American Journal of Public Health*, vol. 83(2), 1993.

Chapman, S, Tobacco and deforestation in the developing world. *Tobacco Control* Vol 3(3), 1994.

Christensen LH. The Non-Smoker Solution. Richmond: Crystal Publishing, 1994.Benowitz L. Cigarette Smoking and Nicotine Addiction. *Medical Clinics of North America*, 76(2): 1992.

DiFranza, JR, Lew, RA. Effect of cigarette smoking on pregnancy complications and sudden infant death syndrome. *The Journal of Family Practice*, Vol. 40, No. 4(Apr), 1995

DiFranza, JR, Lew, RA. Morbidity and Mortality in Children Associated With the Use of Tobacco Products by Other People, *Pediatrics*, Vol. 97, No. 4, April 1996

Ferguson T, *The No-Nag, No-Guilt, Do-It-Your-Own-Way Guide to Quitting Smoking*, Ballantine Books, 1989.

Fiore MC, Jorenby DE, Baker TB, Kenford SL. Tobacco dependence and the nicotine patch: clinical guidelines for effective use. *Journal of the American Medical Association*, Vol. 268(19), 1992.

Fisher EB, Lichtenstein E, Haire-Joshu D, Morgan G, Rehberg HR. Methods, successes, and failures of smoking cessation programs. *Annual Review of Medicine, Vol. 44, 1993.*

Ford B. *Smokescreen: a Guide to the Personal Risks and Global Effects of the Cigarette Habit.* North Perth: Halycon, 1994

Giovino, GA, Henningfield, JE, Tomar, SL, Escobedo, LG, Slade, J. Epidemiology of Tobacco Use and Dependence. *Epidemiologic Reviews*, Vol 17, No. 1, pp 48-65

Haire-Joshu D, Morgan G, Fisher, E, Determinants of Cigarette Smoking. *Clinics in Chest Medicine*, vol. 12(4), 1991.

Health Canada. *Starting and Quitting Smoking* - November 1994. Survey on Smoking in Canada, Cycle 3, Fact sheet No. 5. February 1995.

Huston P. The Benefits of Smoking? *Canadian Medical Association Journal.* 152(2); p 143.

Johnston B, Holtman D, Woods S, Pichera D. Smoking May Be Dangerous To Your Sex Life. *Urological Nursing,* 13(2), 1993.

Klein R, *Cigarettes are Sublime.* Durham and London, Duke University Press, 1993.

Klesges R, DeBon M. *How Women Can Finally Stop Smoking.* Alameda: Hunter House, 1994.

Krogh D. *Smoking: The Artificial Passion.*W.H. Freeman and Co., 1991.

Mackay, J. The Tobacco Problem: Commercial Profit Versus Health – The Conflict of Interests in Developing Countries. *Preventive Medicine* 23, 535-538 (1994)

McBride P, The Health Consequences of Smoking: Cardiovascular Diseases. *Medical Clinics of North America*, 76(2), 1992.

Newcomb P, Carbone P. The Health Consequences of Smoking: Cancer. *Medical Clinics of North America*, 76(2), 1992.

Parrott, AC. Smoking leads to reduced stress, but why? *International Journal of the Addictions*, 30(11), 1509-1516, 1995

Parrott, AC. Stress modulation over the day in cigarette smokers. *Addiction* (1995) 90, 233-244

Peto R, Boreham J, Lopez A, Thun M, Heath C, *Mortality From Smoking in Developed Countries* 1950-2000. Oxford University Press, September 1994.

Prochaska JO, Norcross JC, DiClemente CC. *Changing For Good: The revolutionary program that explains the six stages of change and teaches you how to free yourself from bad habits.* New York: William Morrow, 1994.

Rinpoche S, *The Tibetan Book of Living and Dying*. New York, Harper Collins, 1994.

Royal College of Physicians of London (1992). *Smoking and the Young: A Report of a Working Party of the Royal College of Physicians.* The Lavenham Press Ltd, Great Britain, 1992.

Sacks, JJ, Nelson, DE. Smoking and Injuries: an overview. *Preventive Medicine*, 23, 515-520 (1994)

Samet JM, The Health Benefits of Smoking Cessation. *Medical Clinics of North America*, 76(2).

Schoendorf KC, Kiely JL. Relationship of Sudden Infant Death Syndrome to Maternal Smoking During and After Pregnancy. *Pediatrics*. Vol. 90(6): 1992.

Sherman C, The Health Consequences of Smoking: Pulmonary Diseases. *Medical Clinics of North America*, 76(2), 1992.

United States Environmental Protection Agency. *Respiratory Health Effects of Passive Smoking: Lung Cancer and Other Disorders.* Washington, DC. EPA publication 600/6-90/006F: December 1992.

U.S. Department of Health and Human Services. *Morbidity and Mortality Weekly Report.* Vol. 43(50). 1994.

U.S. Department of Health and Human Services. *The Health Benefits of Smoking Cessation.* A Report of the Surgeon General. DHHS (CDC) Publication No 90-8416, 1990.

U.S. Department of Health and Human Services, Public Health Service. *The Health Consequences of Smoking: Nicotine Addiction.* A Report of the Surgeon General. DHHS (CDC) Publication No 88-8406. 1988.

U.S. Department of Health and Human Services. *Reducing the Health Consequences of Smoking.* A Report of the Surgeon General. DHHS (CDC) Publication No 89-8411, 1989.

Index

Your local bookstore would be happy to serve you.

For your convenience, you may also order by phone from:

BookWorld Services, Inc.
1-800-444-2524
(all major credit cards accepted, 24 hours daily)

...or by fax/mail from publisher using form below:

Name_____

Address   _____

City/town _____

Province/State _____

Postal / Zip code _____

Phone _____fax _____

Please ⟨circle⟩ correct total.

			Canadian residents only please add 7% GST.
1 copy	$16.95 + $3.25	= $20.20	+GST =$21.61
2 copies	$33.90 + $3.25	= $37.15	+GST =$39.75
3 copies	$50.85 + free	= $50.85	+GST =$54.41

U.S. orders please remit same total in U.S funds.
Checks, money orders, or VISA accepted. Payable to:

MiddleWay Publishing Inc,
P.O. Box 70008 (BPO),
Calgary, Alberta,
CANADA T3B 5K3
fax (403) 247-8139
e-mail: sbryant@telusplanet.net

VISA card number _____

Card expiry date _____ / ____

Signature _____

For Additional Copies

Your local bookstore would be happy to serve you.

For your convenience, you may also order by phone from:

BookWorld Services, Inc.
1-800-444-2524
(all major credit cards accepted, 24 hours daily)

...or by fax/mail from publisher using form below:

Name_____

Address   _____

City/town _____

Province/State _____

Postal / Zip code _____

Phone _____fax _____

Please (circle) correct total.

			Canadian residents only please add 7% GST.
1 copy	$16.95 + $3.25	= $20.20	+GST =$21.61
2 copies	$33.90 + $3.25	= $37.15	+GST =$39.75
3 copies	$50.85 + free	= $50.85	+GST =$54.41

U.S. orders please remit same total in U.S funds.
Checks, money orders, or VISA accepted. Payable to:

MiddleWay Publishing Inc,
P.O. Box 70008 (BPO),
Calgary, Alberta,
CANADA T3B 5K3
fax (403) 247-8139
e-mail: sbryant@telusplanet.net

VISA card number _____

Card expiry date _____ / ____

Signature _____